KOOL
ADA

KOOL ADA

Sheila Solomon Klass

SCHOLASTIC
HARDCOVER

Scholastic Inc.
New York

Library of Congress Cataloging-in-Publication Data

Klass, Sheila Solomon,
    Kool Ada / Sheila Solomon Klass.
    p.   cm.
    Summary: When Ada, a tough, street-fighting transplant from coal-mining country to the Chicago slums, gets the no-nonsense Ms. Walker as a teacher, she learns that there are other ways to stand up for yourself.
                        ISBN 0-590-43902-2
    [1. Behavior — Fiction.   2. Teachers — Fiction.   3. City and town life — Fiction.]   I. Title.
PZ7.K67814Ko   1991
[Fic] — dc20   90-40562
                                                   CIP
                                                    AC

12 11 10 9 8 7 6 5 4 3 2 1   1 2 3 4 5 6/9

                    Printed in the U.S.A.   37

            First Scholastic printing, September 1991

In fond memory of
Walka Chavers Paschal,
dear friend and inspired teacher

ONE

"Ada, Ada
Pale Appalachee patater
What kinda stupid name
Is Ada?"

The voice recited that real loud and nasty, and then the elbow hard as a shotgun barrel jammed into my back. It belonged to one of the girls standing in the schoolyard. We were all waiting for the noon dismissal bell. Since this was teachers' meeting day, we only had to come back for one hour in the afternoon. Then we were off Saturday and Sunday, and Monday was a holiday, George Washington's birthday, which made me happy as a hummingbird.

I was skinny. I had no flab or cushioning

1

against that poke in the back, and my worn-out pea coat didn't protect me. I needed an elbow-proof vest. For a second, I just stood there tucking my arms tight to my sides in pain. Then I was ready.

"I hear you're hot to fight, Dummy. Looking for a fight?" The same mean voice. The crowd of kids was streaming out the doorways and all around, pushing and shoving, no one wanting to be last out of the school building. "Scared, hillbilly?"

I knew who it was.

Lizzie.

I didn't have to turn around to see it was the big, red-haired girl in the eighth grade starting up again.

Lizzie two days running. She didn't know me but she saw me around the school — always in trouble — and she figured out that I was from the mountains. That was more than enough for Lizzie. Being born in Chicago made her think that she owned the whole stinking city.

"I don't like hillbillies moving in and messing the place up," she said yesterday before she gave me the punch in my belly. But I stuck my foot out real quick and tripped her up, then I got away.

When somebody did me wrong, I had to stand up to their face. They better know that. Plenty of other kids in our Canaryville neighborhood came from the mountains, but many of them were turning into city people. Trying to. Pretenders. Not me.

Yesterday I tripped her, but yesterday was gone and on this new day I had to do what I had to do. Spinning around, I hit Lizzie right in the soft part of her big puffy nose — hit her twice, two quick ones.

While I was doing it I thought of that Mr. Rogers on TV, and how he would hate for me to do what I was doing. *Mr. Rogers' Neighborhood* is a little kids' program, but I don't care. I'm crazy about Fred Rogers. He's so quiet and smart, always talking about good neighbors.

Lizzie just didn't want to be my neighbor nohow.

There was a thin trickle of blood from Lizzie's nose. She fought me hard, punching wildly with big hammy fists. I didn't waste time. I grabbed hold of a handful of that red hair, frizzy like cotton candy, and I yanked with all my might.

"Lizzie must be high again today," someone said, "if she's picking on a dummy."

"Yeah. She's been looking to fight since first period," another voice answered. They just stood there and watched while she could've killed me.

I wonder what Mr. Rogers and King Friday XIII and Lady Elaine Fairchilde would say about that: she beating me to death while all the other *neighbors* watched, on a beautiful day in our neighborhood.

3

Lizzie dug the nails of her right hand into my cheek. I just held on tighter, and we tumbled to the sidewalk. The girls closed the circle around us so the teachers couldn't see, and I heard the war cry starting up. "Fight! Fight! Fight! Fight! Fight!"

It was over in seconds. Ms. Walker, my new teacher, was suddenly there. She must've cut through that tight crowd clean as a sickle parting high grass. She had us each by the collar and she yanked us up, way way up, so we were dangling like scarecrows off our backsticks. Then she set us down but never let go her hold.

She just stood there, a tall beautiful black woman, looking over the crowd. The girls began to edge back, widening the circle. When she talked her voice was so low, I could hardly hear her. I had to lip-read and I didn't catch the beginning.

" — And that's why I'm really disappointed in you, Ada," she finished grimly.

That very morning she had warned the class to look out for her three dangerous voices. She'd made a list of them on the chalkboard, saying each as she spelled it out.

"CROSS."

"ANGRY."

"FURIOUS."

Then she explained. "CROSS is my natural speaking voice, raised just a bit. ANGRY is loud

4

enough so that the guilty parties and everyone else can hear. FURIOUS, on the other hand, is so faint you'll have to stretch your ears, but it won't matter if you don't hear because you'll know exactly what I mean."

This was FURIOUS.

The unfairness of it bothered me. Lizzie started it. How come Ms. Walker wasn't *really disappointed* in Lizzie? She was an eighth-grader, reared in the city schools. She should have known better.

I put out my lip at the teacher.

Ms. Walker didn't take any notice. She was too busy looking around, noticing the faces, recognizing many of them. "Cora." She nodded as if she were saying how-do. "Nell. Allifair. Grace. Bonnie." The kids in the crowd were mumbling real low. The ones on the outer edge ducked their heads and began to turn away real quick, peeling off like layers of onionskin. "You all run on home now," the teacher advised. "I'll give you till three. Anyone still here after I count to three comes to me at early dismissal this afternoon and stays in the school building for the full day. Arithmetic. Writing. The works."

A lot of them groaned.

She didn't mess around. "One. Two. Three."

Three brought on a stampede. Immediately followed by silence. In the empty schoolyard were the three of us, a one-eyed, ginger-colored cat

5

licking her paws, and the flag up there flapping on the pole. Poor old one-eye. I liked the looks of that cat, but I couldn't go pet her. I didn't dare move. Seemed like that flag rippling was the loudest sound in the world.

Lizzie and I would really get it, I knew. I peeked at Ms. Walker's face, and I could see she wasn't putting on. She was mad, sizzling, hotter than bacon in a skillet. Burning. But she didn't say anything.

I had only been in her class for a couple of weeks, transferred there for my bad attitude: I was a fighter. I didn't speak. I cut school.

The assistant principal, Mrs. O'Neill, who was tall and fat with the biggest knockers in the world, hadn't known where else to put me. "I don't know what to do with you, Ada Garland," she'd fussed. "What's wrong with you, child?" She'd waited a second like she really expected *me* to tell *her*.

I'd stared down at Mrs. O'Neill's feet. They sure were big. She was wearing black open-toed shoes on platforms. Her toes were like little sausages, the toenails painted hot pink!

"Ada, are you listening to me?"

I'd jerked my head up and down, up and down, but I wasn't really. Whenever someone in school began to scold me, I liked to send my mind wandering. Right then I'd been thinking how hard it must be for Mrs. O'Neill to bend over to her sausage-toes to paint the nails. Maybe someone did it for her or else she 'tached the tiny brush to the end of a pointer to reach. This idea was so funny, I'd grinned, and then she got real mad. "Are you trying to wear out my patience, Ada Garland?"

My mouth was zipped up tight, and my face was very serious.

"Well, you've succeeded." She'd breathed a loud breath. "Your stubbornness beats all. We know you used to *talk*. Now I shall *personally* escort you to Ms. Walker's special class for girls to make sure you get there."

Then she'd herded me through the building, she in her shiny, splotchy, black-and-white tight dress, so that everyone saw her alongside me in the halls like a mother Holstein nudging along a maverick calf.

Could be that was when Lizzie took notice of me and decided she would come after me. Could be she just had to take a sniff and she could smell my misery. I was glad I made her nose bleed.

Mrs. O'Neill had led me *personally* to that classroom. I was surprised to see a black teacher because I had never met one before. Aunt Lottie was surprised, too, when I told her. "She's got to be good," Aunt Lottie said. "She's got to be special 'cause it couldn't have been an easy path she walked to get to teach."

Well, I didn't *personally* escort myself back there to her class much afterward. Only when I felt like it. Since I cut school fairly regular, I didn't spend much time with Ms. Walker. But I already understood her better'n any other teacher I ever had.

It wasn't hard. Ms. Walker said what she meant and she meant whatever she said. Every time. She was famous all over the school for that. If she gave her word — promise or punishment — you could count on it. No use pouting, or whining, or apologizing.

"You leave this schoolyard now, Lizzie," Ms. Walker ordered. She could have been chief general of the U.S. Army. "And no waiting around outside, hiding, for when I release Ada," she warned.

I noticed that Lizzie's nostrils were swollen so big she looked a lot like Luella, the pig we had on the farm back home. I really liked Luella. I used to take care to feed her good whenever I could. But I hated this look-alike girl with all the red frizz, standing there rubbing her long painted fingernails over the dark stains on her white satin jacket.

"She's got to pay for the cleaning," Lizzie complained. "She's got blood on my new jacket. Blood don't wash out."

"This is your third fight this week — that I know of, Lizzie — so this is probably old blood. Looks dried to me. You tell Mrs. O'Neill about the stains on your jacket. She'll be expecting you in her office right after lunch." Ms. Walker let go the collar, and Lizzie tried to straighten herself, tight little skirt and all.

"And Lizzie" — the teacher didn't let up — "the next time I catch you picking on a sixth-grader, I'm coming home to do some heavy talking. Now" — she signaled with her thumb sharply like a hitchhiker — "out!"

I listened, and watched, and tried to make sense out of this city life: the big buildings and the crowding, all the different kinds of people, and this school, and just everything. I was shipped up here to my last blood kin in the whole world, my Aunt Lottie, because here is where she lives. And I tried to mind my own business like she told me to.

And then suddenly there would be someone in an alleyway trying to rob me, or on a dark gallery trying to mess with my clothes. Or touch me. Trying to sell grass or smoke or to fight me. Fighting is how it ended up no matter how it started.

Things were so different back home. I was born in a holler tucked in right beside Flat Top Mountain. I'd rather be dead than be born in this ugly, dirty city. Lizzie can have it and welcome to it all.

Where I come from there are woods and birds and fishes and millions of wildflowers: daylilies and red trillium as well as white, bluebells and wood sorrels, rue anemones and saxifrages. Millions for headbands and garlands and bouquets.

9

Mostly people had their own little houses — poor, maybe, nothing fancy but separate — and they kept their own animals and gardens and crops. We raised garden peas and turnips, okra and mushmelons, lettuce and juicy red tomatoes to eat and sell, good stuff we were proud of. In the city it seemed as if the only crops growing were the haters, enemies, coming up faster than weeds.

Lizzie looked right at me. I knew what that look said. It said, I'LL SEE YOU AGAIN!

I stared her back. WHEN YOU SEE ME, I'LL SEE YOU!

Then she took her sweet time shimmying across the schoolyard like Miss Illinois in the Atlantic City Contest they showed on TV. Miss Texas wins, not Miss Illinois. Somebody better tell Lizzie. Miss Illinois is a *big* loser. Especially with fat legs.

"Move it, Lizzie, or you'll park it in the seventh grade for the rest of the year," Ms. Walker warned.

Lizzie speeded up.

Made me grin to hear Ms. Walker talking that way — street talk, not teacher talk — and then see Lizzie hurry.

Ms. Walker looked at me, and I stopped grinning. She let go the collar of my old brown dress, pressing down the bump her fingers raised in the cloth. "I'm disappointed in you, Ada, because

10

you're one of *my* girls, and you heard me say that I don't tolerate fighting in my class. I don't care what others do."

I kept my eyes on her shoes, navy-blue open-back held on with a kind of heel strap, shiny and soft. Oh, wouldn't it be nice to be rich like teachers were! To be tall and thin and have black hair soft and gleaming in the sunlight. To be beautiful the way she was and smart, too, not simple. Then Lizzie and all the other enemies would disappear.

I scraped the toe of my loafer against the pavement. *Tolerate* must mean allow, I worked out in my head. Lots of times if I heard a word used clearly in a sentence, I could figure out the meaning. That way I learned many words from *The Electric Company* and *Sesame Street.* Even some Spanish words. I didn't get to say them, but they were all stored in my head. I liked words even if I couldn't read them. *Tolerate* was a nice one. It had a big sound. Like *splendiferous* and *anticipate.* Important words.

"Are you going to tell me how it started?" Ms. Walker asked.

I shook my head but made no sound. Uh-uh.

For a long time I had no voice at all. It disappeared. Truly. But it didn't matter none. So many terrible things happened to me, I didn't want to talk. When my voice came back from wherever it'd been, I kept it a secret at first. Now I used it only in my house where it was safe.

11

Even if I *was* talking, I'd never tell this teacher that I hated being in her class because it was the Dumbo class. And everyone knew it was Dumbo and made fun of the kids, even though the school tried to hide what it was and pretended it was regular.

It would take a miracle — like the five loaves and two fishes multiplying — to get me a chance to be in a regular class, and then I'd lose Ms. Walker for my teacher and end up never coming to school at all, at all. Never.

Ms. Walker touched the scratches on my cheek. Her fingers were like feathers. "Does it hurt, Ada?" She looked so serious about those scratches. They weren't any big deal.

I shook my head.

"Why did you start with Lizzie?" she asked.

I closed my eyes.

"Anyone can see she's trouble." She smoothed my collar again, waiting.

I opened my eyes and I tried to send my mind traveling away elsewhere so's not to hear her. This time it just wouldn't go. It wanted to hear what she said.

"I've been in this school a long time," she went on, "and I've seen a lot of girls like Lizzie. She's a bomb just waiting to explode. Do you want to be the one who sets her off?" Cupping my chin in her hand, she lifted my face so I had to look right back at her.

She was asking questions that made my tongue ache with answers, but I bit it to keep it still.

"You set her off, and you know who'll get hurt?" she asked.

I stood stiff as a robot, not even blinking. The flag made more flapping noises. Everything else was still.

After a while, she answered her own self. "*You* will. Doesn't matter how good a fighter you are, or how brave you are. Lizzie's got nothing to lose. But you're new here. Just beginning. Don't you want to give yourself a chance?"

Seems this teacher didn't want her lunch. She just had all day to stand there and talk at me. She didn't hurry me along like Mrs. O'Neill. She just took her time.

"Is starting with Lizzie worth risking everything?" Again, she studied my face. "You're smart enough to know the answer is no. So next time, don't start with her.

"To be fair to you, you probably didn't even start this brawl. But you can't take on everyone who comes looking for a fight, either. Sometimes you have to back off. Run away."

She doesn't understand, I thought. Where I come from, we don't back off. We don't run away from anything. We just stand our ground. We're proud folks. This teacher is a city person, prob'ly born right here. Lotsa black folks are city-born.

I stared at her beauty, at the sky-blue soft

dress, glittering gold earrings, and those navy dancing slippers. What could this lady know about enemies?

She was studying me and she seemed to understand what I was thinking. "I don't have answers for outside school," she said to me. "I understand that sometimes you have to fight just to live.

"But in school you must — *must* — stay out of trouble. When it happens, come and tell me. Tell any teacher you can get to. Or run. Run away fast. But don't fight because it will keep you back.

"You've been in the city just about a year now. Right?"

I nodded.

"Look what's happened to you. You hardly come to school and when you do come, you fight. You don't do any schoolwork or homework. No learning at all. That's why you ended up in my special class."

She stopped and waited for me to say something, but I wasn't about to. All those long months I had kept my mouth shut in school, driving them all crazy, so they didn't know what to make of me.

"When the guidance people asked me if I could teach you, I said *yes*," Ms. Walker continued. "I didn't say *maybe*, or *I'll try*. What'd I say?" she asked me.

I didn't answer.

"I said *yes!*" She tapped her foot for emphasis. "I didn't have to accept you. Nobody *made* me take you."

She waited a while, letting that sink in. Then she really came at me. "You want to learn to read and write? And sew? Make your own nice clothes? You want to learn to take your rightful place in this world?"

I couldn't stand it. "I can't," I mumbled. "I'm a ree-tart." I worked on my shoe some more, scuffing it against the pavement. It cost me to say that word. It cost me in my head and in my heart and in the burning place in the back of my eyes. Ree-tart was a very costly word.

Ms. Walker read my mind. "I never use that word. Not because it's a bad word. Because it makes my girls sound different from other people, and I don't think they are."

I blinked fast. My eyes were burning hot the way they used to long ago before Pa died, when happenings really hurt me.

"It's nice to hear your voice, Ada. I knew you could talk. I just wondered when you'd stop playing that silence game. You've been at it a long time. You know something? You've got a sweet voice." She paused, but then went on. "You *can* learn, Ada. I know about such things. That's my job. I promise, you can."

I stayed quiet. It wasn't any use talking. Not as long as there were new crops of enemies coming up every day.

"Stay out of fights so you can come along on the trip we're planning to the zoo. Fighters can't go on trips. It's entirely up to you. Would you like to go to the Lincoln Park Zoo?"

I bobbed my head up and down, yes, yes, I would, I surely would.

"Good. And Ada — do the homework I assigned this morning. You have the whole long weekend for it. I'm going to especially look for yours. Now run home and wash those scratches clean with soap and water. You'll barely have time to eat."

I took off. No Miss-America-Contest wiggling for me. I ran. I turned back once when I came to the gate of the schoolyard and I was surprised to see Ms. Walker still standing there, looking after me.

She lifted her long arm to wave good-bye.

I didn't wave back, but I felt pretty happy.

Standing tall and straight there, she looked like a chocolate Statue of Liberty, I thought. Only prettier. Much prettier.

My teacher!

TWO

I was racing up the stairs, needing to wash the blood and dirt out of the scratches. I saw someone in the shadows on the second-floor landing where the bulb was out. Folks kept stealing the bulbs from out of the hallway. He was facing away from the little light there was.

"Want to buy some crack?" he asked, grinning like one of those pumpkin-faces missing teeth. He was a new one. I never saw him around before. He was about my age or maybe a little older but not much.

I slipped my foot out of my shoe and grabbed the shoe up in my hand. "Aaai!" I screamed, real loud, and I thumped the shoe on the banister as I backed down away from him. Then again I screamed even louder, "Aaai! Aaai!"

Of all the people in the city, I hated them the

worst, the dealers who were turning so many folks on the streets into enemies, my enemies and Aunt Lottie's and even enemies to themselves, getting sick and puking or being mean or acting just plain dopey; crowds of them standing lopsided or sitting nodding on the sidewalks, almost dead, with their eyes blinking like broken traffic lights.

"*Sh*. Whatsamatter? You chicken?" The kid made a move down one step toward me.

I knew I'd rather be a live chicken than a dead duck. Again I raised my voice, making the loudest noise I could.

A lock clicked on someone's door. The dealer froze. He thought my yelling was bringing family to help me. He was down the stairs and out the door fast as if a rattler was nipping at his skinny butt. Which I wished it was.

I was real pleased as I went up the rest of the stairs. I might be a lady cop one day and go after dealers. I straightened up and tried to walk tall. I'd be like Lacey, smart and tough. "Dealers, get lost!" I whispered my wish as I turned the key in my lock.

While I was washing, I tried to figure out a way to hide the scratches for when I went back to school, and for later when I went downstairs to check out the McCoys' health, something I did every afternoon first thing after I arrived home.

Mr. and Mrs. McCoy, the supers of our beat-up building, are very old. It seemed a miracle to me that they weren't dead. Mr. McCoy liked to tease me by saying they'd come from Kentucky more than twenty-five years ago, and they'd stayed alive just to welcome me when it was my turn to come from the mountains. Each morning when I woke up, with Aunt Lottie already gone to work, first thing I wondered was if Mr. and Mrs. McCoy would still be there when I came downstairs to visit. It was hard for me to wait till afternoon to get into the basement and check. Even when I played hooky I had to wait because I couldn't show myself before the end of school hours.

Lucky I could check on Aunt Lottie easy, as many times a night as I wanted to. I just tiptoed into the bedroom doorway and listened for her breathing noises. The best nights were when she snored, loud funny snores that came flying into the living room where I made the davenport my bed. Those nights I didn't need to worry for a minute. I didn't have to stay up and watch the late-night movies to keep from being scared. Those snorey nights I slept a sweet sleep without any bad dreams.

It was Death I was on the watch for.

In a sermon, Preacher once declared, "We must love and support one another, for love brings warmth and shelter." Then his voice got deep and scary: "And Death is a cold cold wind!"

and I shivered and my teeth chattered because I knew it was true. When I was little, that cold wind blew round me so often it made me numb. My mind learned to move far off, to take shelter whenever that wind blew. That way it couldn't cut into me so deep each time.

The cold wind carried away my mother a minute after I was born, and it took my brother Will Junior when he was nine.

"Newmonia," the district nurse said, but I knew that it was the cold cold wind.

Will Junior was my playmate and my best and closest friend. He used to make me so proud letting me walk to school on the road aside him. He was tall and had a face very much like mine and Pa's, thin and pale with bright blue eyes, a straight little nose, light silky blond hair, and a smile so big and friendly folks couldn't help but smile right back at him.

He skipped fourth grade he was so smart. "My Will's going to be something," Pa told everyone. "He's really got a head on him." And it was true. That same year, Will Junior won the Sunday school spelling bee by getting the bonus word — leviathan — right on the very first spell. All the kids clapped and clapped, and I clapped so hard my hands tingled. He loved words and he was teaching me how to love them, too. Words and rhymes. Will Junior could rhyme most anything. Rhyming was a sound game we played as we fished in the creek or hunted mushrooms and berries on the mountainside. The best rhyme Will ever made was on my ninth birthday. He put it on a cardboard with a cutout picture of red roses he got somewhere.

> *Being nine is mighty fine, Ada*
> *But being ten will be even greater!*

I loved that rhyme. I said it to myself over and over. I couldn't wait till I was ten, and he wrote me something again.

Will Junior wasn't there by the time I got to ten.

When he died, a big empty space opened up in the world — a hole. I kept looking for him in the woods, in the fields, on the mountain, everywhere, for a long time afterward because it just seemed impossible that Will could not be around somewhere. But there was only empty space. I used to talk to Will Junior out loud whenever there was no one else around to hear. I needed him to know I missed him, and Pa was having a mighty hard time because he missed him, too, and Pa had no work and he was coughing all through the nights. Time passed and I got to where I could almost manage without thinking about my brother. I wasn't moping all the time or crying. I hardly talked to him out loud any more.

Then in the new year, the creek froze solid in its deep bed, and the cold wind came crashing back. Late one moonless night, it shook our cabin and whistled in through the cracks where we had rags and papers stuffed. That wind battered at the door, wailing outside like a banshee, and it blew my Pa away forever.

"Breathing troubles," the district nurse said this time. "Black lung." Pa had picked up the cough working in the mines, and he never did get completely well.

Then the nurse leaned over to pull up that sheet and cover all of Pa, even his face.

"No!" I screamed, but my scream didn't come out with any sound. Just a stretched-open mouth. I reached up to stop her, but she took hold of my hand hard and pulled me away from Pa's bed. "Ada, you got no one here now," she said. "You got to go to your grandaunt in Chicago." She dropped her checkered shawl on my shoulders, but I couldn't stop my trembling. "Hear?" she asked. She pulled up that sheet forever.

I didn't answer her.

"Ada?"

I couldn't. I just couldn't. That was when I just stopped listening to words. The sounds of folks talking bounced around in the air outside my understanding.

I didn't cry for Pa like I did for Will Junior. My

chest was filled with heavy rocks of ice. I stopped listening. I took shelter in the cave of my mind where it was warm and safe. I just sat and sucked my thumb and bit my cuticles until they bled. I stopped talking and I lived back inside my head where I was a little bit protected.

When they sent me up on the bus to this big terrible city, my mind kept to its shelter. In there I could do anything I want, make up stories and even play at rhymes. My favorite made-up city story was: *Once upon a time there was a cold wind that blew too fast. It blew so fast it blew past the McCoys' house in Kentucky and Aunt Lottie's little house in the holler, and it missed both houses in its big chilly hurry. Now it's looking all over for them and howling like a banshee, but it can't ever find them because they're here in this big city. That's how come Mr. and Mrs. McCoy and Aunt Lottie got to be so old. They were spared by the stupid old hurrying wind.*

It was true that the bad veins in Aunt Lottie's legs sometimes bulged like blue ropes and hurt her something fierce, but she always chided me, "Nobody ever died of veins, child. Don't you fret about me."

I believed the Lord was keeping Aunt Lottie down here below to do His work, to love Him and His church. Her particular job seemed to be to watch that things were kept spick-and-span, to inspect the dust and dirt clear off the earth.

Mr. McCoy was the one who taught me what to do on the stairs when that dealer came at me. "Get away from those rats fast," he advised me. "Bang. Make a noise. Run. Yell. Punch. Kick. You know, Ada, I'm always saying you're too hot, too ready to fight. Well, that's true — 'cept when a drug dealer is around. Then you just be hot, Ada. Scream! Hit him if you have to, or kick him in his privates. Anything. But get away! Don't let him talk you into using stuff. No listening to sweet words about trying something one time, what can it hurt. No tasting any free samples!"

Mr. McCoy knew what he was talking about. Didn't his wife, Jen, have a niece up from near the Tug Fork, Kentucky, side, and didn't she die of an overdose a few years back? Her mother — Jen's favorite sister, Thelma — was still suffering fainting spells and crying out of sadness till she could hardly see. In the city one week and dead. ONE WEEK!

Mr. McCoy wanted to protect me. "You are a fatherless mite," he'd tell me. "A puny, fatherless mite. Got to put some meat on your bones. Got to get you to talk up instead of using your fists all the time. Got to look after you."

When Fred Rogers gets to be real old, he's going to be like Mr. McCoy. They both already wear cardigan sweaters. Mrs. McCoy says that's what you call the ones with the zippers up the front.

I looked at my face in the mirror.

The scratches were bad but not terrible. Three red ant tracks ran from just above my left ear to my cheekbone. They were deepest where they started over the ear, which was mighty lucky because my long hair would cover them if I combed it real smart.

I scrubbed the scratches with soap and water. The soap made them sting worse than when Lizzie first dug her nails in, but I kept scrubbing hard, figuring the worse the sting the cleaner the soap was making it. Then I dried my face and used a little of the zinc ointment Aunt Lottie had bought for me when I fought before. It was on the shelf right by the sink, handy, and that was lucky because I didn't want to tell her about fighting in school. Last, I brushed my hair forward so it hung loose over my cheeks.

I ate my peanut-butter sandwich and my apple and drank my milk fast, all the while thinking about the homework. It wasn't just regular copying exercises that the teachers usually gave: COPY TEN SENTENCES AND FILL IN THE MISSING WORDS. No, none of that. Ms. Walker had told us, "Go home and look in the mirror. Really look at yourselves and make a list of your good points. Think about the important parts of yourself. Write down a list of what you see that you like." My teacher thought up interesting assignments.

*   *   *

I got back to school late and slipped right into my seat, so no one had a chance to look at me up close. My hair was spread like a tent over my face. We did arithmetic until it was almost time for the teachers' meeting, and then Ms. Walker began to remind everyone about the homework.

But she was looking directly at me!

I hadn't said one word in class, so nobody knew I could talk 'cept Ms. Walker. Several times when I knew a subtraction answer, I almost wanted to raise my hand, but I didn't. It was too hard to begin.

"Ada," the teacher said. "Ada, would you repeat the assignment?"

It was so quiet in that room, you could have heard a ladybug walking. Then someone giggled, and there were a bunch of whispers and hushing noises.

"Teacher — " Yolanda called out. That was what she did most in class. Call out.

"Ms. Walker."

"Ms. Walker — Ada can't talk."

"Ada?" Ms. Walker tilted her head to one side and waited that way.

The room got very still again.

My throat was dry, and my tongue was a balloon in my mouth. I wanted so much to say it right. I started very slowly. "We have to make a list" — I stopped to breathe — "of all the parts of ourself we like."

26

Yolanda sure looked funny with her mouth hanging open. LaVerne, a nice black girl who wore three hairbows sometimes, began to clap her hands and jump up in her seat. "She can talk! Ada can talk good as anyone! Yay, Ada!"

Then Maureen, who was very tall and a copycat, said it, too, "Yay, Ada!" and she clapped, and some others joined in.

My face was hot, and I didn't know where to look, so I looked back at the teacher. She was clapping hard.

"Right," she said. "You gave the assignment exactly right."

Aunt Lottie had a long mirror nailed to the door. She must've put it there years ago when she first came to the city because it had black puddles in a few places, but mostly it was a clear mirror. After studying myself in this glass, I made a list in my head of what I was seeing. I did what the teacher said. I really looked at myself. And I saw:

skinny legs
skinny arms
straight long yellow raggedy hair
no bust
no behind

No good important parts to put on my list.
I considered my eyes, which are blue and were

doing the looking at me. They were okay but nothing special. Maureen, in my class, had bigger blue eyes and she had dark eyelashes. My pale skin didn't have pimples, and my teeth were pretty even and white — not like that pumpkin-face dealing drugs in the hallway — but teeth and skin were not the *important* parts. The most important part in my class was to need a bra and I didn't. Some of the girls in the class were already wearing B cups. Like Giant Jessica, who was always showing off.

"B is for Big — " Jessica bragged whenever she wore her red sweater. She was always poking out her breasts like she just bought them and they were a big deal, two for the price of one, on Maxwell Street.

But I was flat, an ironing board, and there wasn't a sign of anything growing whenever I looked. I looked every night. It didn't make sense. Mrs. O'Neill, the assistant principal, was probably a size Z cup — more than she could ever need — and I wouldn't even get to A. Or AA.

"Making a list might be easy for *you*, Ms. Beautiful Teacher," I told the empty bathroom. "You got plenty of things to put down. You'd be writing for an hour or more." I spent a lot of time thinking about Ms. Walker.

She was a very tall woman, not so young, I guess — her black hair was beginning to turn gray near her forehead and face — but she wasn't really old like Aunt Lottie and the McCoys.

No. Ms. Walker was nowhere near that kind of old. She was in between. Where we lived there weren't so many in-betweens. Seemed as if people rushed from being young to being old without waiting a while in the middle so you could see them. Movie stars and TV people stayed young a long time, and then they stayed in between a very long time, it seemed right up till they died. They never did get *old*. Most likely there was some secret formula. Like the Geritol that Aunt Lottie took, only stronger. And costly.

For a lady who wasn't old, Ms. Walker sure was finicky. Especially about her title. On the board in the classroom, she had printed in big letters — MS. WALKER. Some days I could read the name clearly. Other times the letters wouldn't stay put exactly. But I always knew it said MS. WALKER. I couldn't read or spell right, but I could remember.

"This is what you will call me," the teacher told the class three, four times. "*Ms.* just means grown woman. It doesn't mean married. That's *Mrs.* It doesn't mean single. That's *Miss*.

"Ms. will be your title — yes, each one of you — when you're past sixteen or so. Get used to hearing it and using it. A lady's title shouldn't depend upon whether or not she's married. She's a lady whether she's married or not. What you call a person is very important to her and to you.

What you call her is how you think of her."

All that talk and fuss over what to call her. That teacher was set on people doing things exactly right. Big things, little things, all exactly right.

If I could be anyone in the world, I thought, going back to look in the mirror one more time, I'd be Ms. Walker. I'd be tall and beautiful and smart. The best teacher in the school. Maybe in the world. My eyes would see right into a person and make them tell the truth.

Second, I'd be Madonna.

Third, I'd be —

I couldn't choose third.

I picked up two apples and put them in the top pockets of my old brown dress, and then I stood tiptoe to see the whole effect if I had high heels on. It didn't help none. The apples just made funny bumps.

What Ms. Walker said about coming regular to school made some sense. But —

I couldn't go back Tuesday.

Not because of Lizzie.

Because of the homework.

I just couldn't make up a list of my good points. And I didn't want to hear Jessica's list. I'll bet it was longer than the telephone book.

THREE

I moved silently down the cellar steps, two at a time, like a spy. Just as I'd hoped, there was Mr. McCoy, *alive*, still pushing his brush-broom along the dark stone floor. The pipes along the ceiling kept the place wonderfully warm and made soft hissing noises. I stopped on the third step from the bottom and waited.

Did he hear me? Surely not this time. I was super soft-feet herself.

"Is that some space invader?" he called out.

"No. No space invader. It's only Ada."

I made the jump and landed neatly right beside him. We always played this game. No matter how quiet I was, he always guessed I was there.

"Got you again, Ada," he said and he chuckled. "My eyes don't see so good, but my ears are better than a young deer's."

31

His eyeglasses, the thickest I ever saw, shone in the cellar lights, and even wearing glasses he couldn't make out the small trash on the ground. I helped him. He was my first and best friend in the city, and I trusted him. Every day except Sunday, he wore blue overalls and a blue work shirt just like Pa had done. Looking at him took me back to everything: Pa, the holler, Will Junior, Flat Top Mountain, Luella the pig.

The broom was not moving. Mr. McCoy was leaning on it. He was strong and healthy but a little stiff because he was old. He looked me over. "Ada? You been fighting?" He sure was smart.

I shook my head.

"You sure?"

I nodded. If I didn't actually say anything, it wasn't as big a lie.

I had brushed my soft loose hair over my scratched cheek again, spreading it thin so he wouldn't be able to see any marks.

"Then you didn't bother to comb your hair today. A pretty little thing like you with your hair looking like a rat's nest. What a shame. Wish I had hair. You'd see. I wouldn't only comb it neat, but I'd color it butter-color like yours and put it in rollers." He moved his fingers in curling motions around his head to show me. We both burst out laughing. Mr. McCoy hadn't a single hair on his head.

32

He didn't say anything more about the way I looked. Most likely he didn't see the big rip in my sleeve where Lizzie had pulled hard. But even if he noticed the rip and the wrinkled dress, the wonderful thing about Mr. McCoy was that he didn't go on about things.

This wasn't true of any other living grown-up. It had been true of Pa. He could leave off scolding. But not Aunt Lottie or Preacher or Jen McCoy. Certainly not the Sisters of the church. When they saw something they didn't approve of, they speechified — if there is such a word. Anyway, that's what they did. When Mr. McCoy saw something about me he didn't like, he was quiet. Sometimes, later on, he'd talk about it, but no speeches. "You're home kind of early today, Ada. Did you cut school this afternoon to watch TV and to visit down here?"

"No, Mr. McCoy. I wouldn't do that ever again."

"Good thing," he said. "That one time I had to listen to your Aunt Lottie a whole hour preaching hellfire and damnation. That woman don't belong working in a restaurant kitchen, you know. She belongs in the *pul*pit. Yessir. Why, I didn't have to run the furnace that night, she heated up this old place so with her talk. Making me sound like the evil Coachman in that *Pinocchio* story, luring you away from school."

Luring. That must mean doing tricks and using

magic. Like using the pretty fish-lures to fool the fish. I grinned at the idea of Mr. McCoy being that Coachman. Not that he couldn't handle horses 'cause he used to back in the country, but he wasn't evil at all.

He was the one who noticed in the *TV Guide* that *Pinocchio* was going to be on, and he told me. He watched for all the good programs for me: the Grinch, and Yertle, and Charlie Brown. Mr. McCoy would make a great Gepetto, but no Coachman. No way. He admired learning. He would have made Pinocchio go to school every single day, even in rain and snow.

"I didn't cut school. Today was a short day."

He smiled a big smile that showed most of his wonderful even false teeth. China. That's what he called them. Once, he took them out to show me how they worked. I wished Aunt Lottie would get such teeth, so it would be easy for her to chew. She had only a few teeth left and had to soak everything in coffee or soup or gravy before she could eat.

But when I told her that Mr. McCoy had these beautiful teeth that I admired so, Aunt Lottie said that caring about such things was vanity and a sin.

She was paying for a fine stone for Pa's grave.

"Short day, huh?" Mr. McCoy thought that was a funny idea. "Wish I was a teacher. Supers don't ever get short days."

"You don't want to be a teacher," I told him, picking up the dustpan. "Teachers are mostly uptight."

"Lucky for me I don't want to be one, I guess, because I don't have enough learning to teach a flea to fly."

"Oh, you're real smart, Mr. McCoy," I said. "You could learn anything you wanted to real easy."

He looked at me over the top of his big thick black-rimmed glasses. "You're not doing it so easy, girl. Or else you wouldn't be staying out of school so much. All those wasted days. All that keeping still like you're dumb — " He shook his head, then bent slightly to brush the trash up into my pan. I scooped it up and tossed it into the barrel.

"You're very smart, Mr. McCoy. You know all about so many things, plumbing and electric work and everything. Aunt Lottie says that you're the best warrior the Lord ever created in the battle against roaches. She says you're just plain outnumbered, but you're fighting the good fight."

"Your aunt speaks gospel," Mr. McCoy said, mighty pleased. "I told you she could be a preacher." Together we moved through the basement, past garbage cans and stored furniture spooky under sheets, finishing the cleanup, then we put the broom and dustpan away.

"How come you won't settle down in school

and learn, Ada? I've been wanting to ask you that for a long time. School can be a big help in this life. It can keep the streets from chewing up a person for good."

"I'm a ree-tart," I told him. "That means I can't learn."

"That's a false label put on the product," Mr. McCoy said, his wrinkled face getting red all the way up over his shiny scalp. "Going to report them to the Better Business Bureau. Who dared use that word on you?"

It hurt me to tell him. Ree-tart is an ugly name, and Mr. McCoy didn't care for what he called *language*. He didn't use it himself.

Lizzie used the word as a fighting curse. And I heard the assistant principal, Mrs. O'Neill (old moo-cow), whisper it to the lady working the typewriter in her office before she *personally* marched me to Ms. Walker's class. The school people always *whispered* it or didn't say it at all. They only looked at you and thought it. It meant dumber than the dumbest ones.

I would have to try to explain to Mr. McCoy. "Mostly they don't say the word out loud. They just give everyone a bunch of printed tests, hard tests, real hard, then they mark them, and they sort the kids out according to how dumb they are. End of the year, they put the ree-tarts in special classes. I got put in one in the middle of the year because I never talk and a lot of other reasons."

"Don't use the word, eh? Just like they don't know what to use when they're talking to us sometimes. They'll say 'you people' whenever they mean us. They'd like to say hillbillies, but they're scared to. I've been a 'me people' in a government office more times than I can count. Say, I bet I know what they call your class. They must call it the 'you people' class."

He always turned pain around somehow and made me laugh.

"No, they just gave us a number for our name. The kids in the class say they switch the number or the letter or whatever every couple of years so no one can tell for sure if she's in the ree-tart class. But everyone always knows. I heard LaVerne — a girl in my class — say she used to be in the 'ceptional children's class in another school. What does that mean, Mr. McCoy?"

"Means special. Something real special. I'd like for someone to call me 'Exceptional Super.' "

"Not in school you wouldn't like it. Everyone there wants to be regular. Not special anything."

Mr. McCoy scratched over his left ear awhile, considering this problem. He ended up shaking his head. He was a stubborn man. "Ada — I didn't live all these years without learning a few things, and one of the few things I can tell is a person's smartness. You got a good enough head to learn lots of things once you want to." He fell silent for a bit. "You just didn't get proper chances. So you stopped wanting to try and got left way behind. Maybe you'll never catch up all the way, but how I see it is not everyone has to be a big brain. Some of us got to be just plain George" — he tapped his own chest — "and Jen." He pointed to his apartment door. "And I give thanks for what I am."

"You've almost got a rhyme, Mr. McCoy."

"I do?"

"We are just plain George and Jen
We thank the Lord for that. Amen."

"Nice. See — there's nothing wrong inside your head. You're all right in there, Ada, no matter what troublesome folks say."

His kind words fell on my ears like a blessing. Aunt Lottie never said praising things like that to me. Mr. McCoy once explained that Aunt Lottie really feared the evil eye. Since I already had so much trouble in my life, she was trying to protect me by not attracting evil forces. He, himself, didn't believe in the evil eye. "All that stuff is stupidstitions," he liked to say, and make Jen mad because she believed in some of it.

"Mr. McCoy," I told him, "some of the kids in my class are thirteen, and they're so simple they can't even tell their own name and address. It's the slowest sixth-grade class in the galaxy." I got that word from *Star Trek*.

He let out a long whistle. "You sure must've worked at being ornery to get yourself put in there," he said, "because there is absolutely no dee-fect in your head. None. How'd you manage it, Ada?"

"Attitude. Mrs. O'Neill, the assistant principal, who looks like a Holstein cow that's had good grazing, called it an attitude."

"You don't have any different attitude than others, " he scoffed, "unless you told her about her cow resemblance."

I shook my head. I never said a single word out loud to her.

"That word *attitude* doesn't mean anything."

He really didn't understand, so I had to tell him. "When I first came, I had the biggest attitude in the whole school. You remember, first I couldn't talk and then when I could, I wouldn't talk. Not even to the bossy man in the white coat like they wear in the supermarket. He was trying to get me to see things on some ink-blotty cards. Some of the blots looked like the black puddles in Aunt Lottie's mirror, but I didn't even tell him that. My mouth was zipped. It'd still be that way except today Ms. Walker tricked me into talking. She is so-o smart. She's too smart to be a teacher."

"How'd she trick you?"

"Well" — I couldn't explain exactly — "she stopped me fighting, and she didn't yell none or punish me. She just talked to me nice and said if I want, I could learn to read and write and sew."

"See! That's the ticket. What'd I tell you? She knows you can learn."

"She said she would help me — " My voice shook. "Mr. McCoy, I *can't* read good any more. Will Junior was teaching me, and I used to try, but my head doesn't stay reliable now. Sometimes I look and the letters are all regular letters. They make words. Other times I look and I see the shapes and lines, but they don't make words for me."

Mr. McCoy looked bewildered. "Maybe you need glasses, Ada. Like me."

"No. They gave me an eye test in gym, and I passed it just fine. I saw all the shapes on the chart. They're big and separated. But when they're words, some days they're nothing to me."

"Well, this kind of trouble is news to me, but if you tell that smart teacher all of this — she went to college — probably it's not anything too hard for her to figure out.

"Come on," he said. "You've got to give it a try. You're a tough little one, Ada." He smiled at me. "And you're going to be a credit to 'us people.' "

"I have to go upstairs now, Mr. McCoy," I said.

"I've got a lot of work to do before Aunt Lottie gets home."

"Well, you just run on up and do your chores and watch your TV. Don't be worrying too much about this re-tard nonsense. You're smarter than many. Anyone doesn't believe that, you just send him right to George McCoy."

He made me feel so much better. I was very lucky to have Mr. McCoy for my neighbor.

"But it doesn't come easy, Ada. You've got to go to school and work at learning. You've got to talk and listen to others and think. Smartness isn't born in people. It's collected. They just go buzzing around, gathering it up from everywhere same as the bees gather pollen, and they turn it into honey. There's nothing sweeter than smartness you gathered up yourself."

He was an *exceptional* explainer.

I was happy. I took giant steps up the stairs, three at a time, until I was safe in my own apartment, the door locked. While I made the place orderly, I thought about what Mr. McCoy had said to me. It was a lot to think about.

He was right. There was a kind of sweetness to sitting there thinking about things all by myself in the quiet. In a way I felt close to Will Junior.

FOUR

On February twenty-second, as soon as I opened my eyes and saw it was ten o'clock, I closed them again and I gave thanks. I knew it wasn't Thanksgiving, but I gave thanks that I got to sleep late and that George Washington was born. His birthday was what made the twenty-second a super celebration.

I lay on my pull-out bed warm and cosy under the Jacob's ladder patchwork quilt Aunt Lottie had made when she was a young woman. She was one good seamster. I snuggled there, my toes all tangled up in that bedding, remembering that my Pa had slept under this same quilt when he was a boy and came visiting Aunt Lottie during planting time back home. "When he came to help in the fields," Aunt Lottie said, a remembering smile on her face, "your Pa Will always favored this quilt." So Pa and I both shared the Jacob's Ladder, perfect little white and colored squares running up and back a million times. And soft!

I had oceans of time to idle this morning. So first I went over the list of blessings the day brought.

1. No school
2. No Lizzie to fight
3. Mr. McCoy's birthday party

Aunt Lottie was working, but she'd be home one hour early.

On the table was the present all ready. Aunt Lottie and I took a long time to wrap it just perfectly last night. She had crocheted a thick wool gray cardigan sweater, and now it was hidden in the thinnest white tissue paper in a shiny blue box with a gorgeous orange bow on it. The bow came ready-made. Next to the present, covered by a paper towel to keep it clean, was the birthday card I'd drawn. I used Magic Markers Ms. Walker lent me to draw a picture of Mr. McCoy in his overalls. In my picture he was smiling so all his china showed, and he was bald-headed like he really is. Anyone, even a fool, could tell it was Mr. McCoy.

Washington's Birthday was really Mr. McCoy's adopted birthday. He was born before most everything important was around: TVs, Walkmen, colored movies, McDonald's, ballpoint pens. When Mr. McCoy went to grade school, he had to dip his penholder in a little glass inkwell in his desk, he says. Sometimes he dipped the long braid of the girl sitting in front of him, too. For devilment. After the first big world war was when he was born, but he couldn't swear to exactly when.

"How could you lose your birthday, Mr. McCoy?" I wondered. "I know when mine is."

He thought about it awhile. "They didn't bother much with writing things down in those days, Ada. Didn't seem too important, I guess. I was the eighteenth baby to come along in my family. Maybe they got tired of writing them all down."

According to Mr. McCoy, he never had one single birthday till he married Jen, and then she chose one for him.

"Might as well have a birthday like every other civilized person," Jen had said. "Might as well be Washington's birthday, so it will stay fixed in folks' minds. Your name is George, and you've already missed too many birthdays. You don't want to miss any more."

Mr. McCoy took to the idea. "I was a February-blizzard baby," he'd said. "The midwife couldn't make it through the snow. So the twenty-second might well be the day. Near enough, anyway. And I *never* told a lie in my life." He crossed his fingers high in the air while he'd said that.

Jen had laughed at him, and the date was set.

Once they took to celebrating it every year, Jen says, the government began monkeying with Washington's Birthday, shifting it around.

I couldn't understand how you could change someone's birthday after he was born and lived and died.

"Convenience," Jen said. "They're making long weekends." But that didn't explain it.

"We'll stick with the twenty-second." Jen made up her mind. "If they move Washington's Birthday to another time, we'll stay to our day. Someone's got to celebrate it. They can just take their Presidents Day and do it in June for all I care."

Part of Mr. McCoy's birthday celebration each year was a three-layered cake — not one, not two, but three layers — covered with soft cherry frosting the exact color of the blossoms.

On February twenty-second last year, I had only been up from the country about five weeks, scared, trembling all the time so I couldn't stand still or sit still, and feeling so lost I only wanted to disappear. I wasn't talking to anyone in those days; I had no voice.

The McCoys invited me to that birthday, and I came, carrying Aunt Lottie's present, a long red wool muffler and a stocking hat to match, which Mr. McCoy immediately put on and wore all during the party, saying it was mighty cold in the basement and this woolen hair substitute was better than a wig. "Just call me Red," he'd said.

45

I was served two helpings of birthday cake. I'd never had so much cake in my life. Never.

Then they gave me the spatula to lick.

That was when I tried to say my very first words in Chicago. My very first words since I went to wake Pa up that terrible cold morning and he wouldn't wake, and the district nurse came and said "black lung," and she reached for the sheet to cover him all up, and I couldn't scream the word "NO!" hard as I tried.

Jen handed me that spatula piled with pink frosting. She gave it to me carefully so not a bit would drop off, and I took it and moved my mouth, trying my best to whisper, "Thank you, Jen."

"Praise God!" Aunt Lottie sang out when she saw me trying, and she picked her heavy self up out of the chair and came round to hug me. "This child is gonna be all right!" She squeezed me close to her. She was so warm!

I was happy she was hugging me, of course, but I worried about her knocking some of the icing onto the floor. I began to lick it, and I thought about the word *spatula* and what a fine thing it was with little openings for icing to pile into. I hadn't heard it but that one time. The sound of it stayed in my head. It was a special party word.

By the time I'd licked it clean, I figured out that it might be possible to live in this ugly old city.

Just so long as I didn't have to talk outside the house. Where the cold wind blew. And enemies grew. An ugly rhyme. I hated it.

In the months since that birthday, I became good friends with Jen, too. Jen was even older and stiffer than Mr. McCoy. I loved her small-ness. She was not even five feet tall, a neat, spare, pale-skinned woman with white hair swirled like cotton. Just opposite from my aunt, who was so big-boned. Some days when I was downstairs talking to Mr. McCoy, Jen would swing open the kitchen door of their basement apartment and call to me to help. "Bending jobs," she'd say. "Anyone out there willing to take on a bending job?"

I would dust the wall molding or take things out of the low cupboards or pick up things that had fallen. Jen always rewarded me with some-thing nice. Mostly she gave me hot crullers fresh out of her skillet or handfuls of soft raisins or big chunks of cheese.

"This is better'n money," she'd say. "I don't believe in giving children money for helping out."

I figured the real reason was Mr. and Mrs. McCoy didn't have money. Aunt Lottie said they got their apartment free for caring for the building. Mr. McCoy was once a seaman. He sailed all over the world and worked at many different jobs — all kinds — but he was too old for that now. Sometimes he'd speak his mind out. "Where'll we be when I can't push this broom around any more?"

If Jen was around, she'd stop that kind of talk by telling him, "The Lord will provide."

Jen belonged with Aunt Lottie to the Church of the Holy Light, and both of them were always giving answers like that to hard questions.

How would the Lord provide? I wondered.

Aunt Lottie said asking questions like that one was sass. A person just had to believe without thinking up smart-ass questions.

It was confusing to me.

I couldn't figure out how the Lord would provide if Lizzie was waiting on a corner. I would have to handle *that* myself.

I'll handle it, I told myself. I can beat up Lizzie. She's just an old ball of city blubber. I could sneak up on her and punch her nose again. I could hit her in the teeth. I could wear rings from soda cans on all my fingers and break her mouth.

If I hide from her, she'll find me out. She'll be waiting. She'd looked at me, and that look said I'LL SEE YOU AGAIN!

If there's another fight in school, Ms. Walker will put me out of the class. She won't tolerate me no more. She don't tolerate fighters. I won't get to go on the trip to Lincoln Park. To the zoo.

But if I fight her in the street, Ms. Walker will know anyway. She gets to know practically every-

48

thing that is going on, even if she's far away from it. She says she has eyes all over, and I believe it.

If I could die quick like Pa, I'd just lay me down under the beautiful Jacob's ladder quilt and turn out the light and sleep and never wake up. That way wouldn't hurt a bit. That way would burn Lizzie. She wouldn't have a chance to get even.

Bet if I died, Aunt Lottie would pray her head off real loud. Wonder God don't get a headache from all that loud praying. When Aunt Lottie gets the Spirit, hold your ears!

Mr. McCoy would be sad. Bet he'd cry. It hurts his eyes, he says, to cry because he once had something bad — cat tracks — in his eyes and they had to be taken out in a big operation. That was when he went to a government office for help to pay for the operation and they 'you peopled' him near to death.

Jen would be heartbroken. It would be like her niece, Thelma's girl, all over again.

I guess I better stay alive and not make sadness for everyone. There's nothing wrong with my breathing anyhow.

I'll get Lizzie before she gets me.

Then Ms. Walker will send home a note for Aunt Lottie to come. Aunt Lottie will read it carefully and slowly and then she'll put that note away safe in her drawer with her Bible and her gravestone receipt and all her other important papers. And she'll look at me real sad and make her regular speech.

"I pray for you all the time, child, and I ask our Redeemer to help you because you sure had enough trouble already. How come you don't want to learn?"

I couldn't explain it to her.

I *did* want to learn. There were so many things I wanted to know. So many! But in school nobody cared about what kids wanted to know. They were teaching us what *they* wanted us to know. It was boring. Sometimes I just fell asleep sitting there. Nobody minded because what they really wanted was for all the kids to sit still and be quiet. Sleeping was the quietest way I could be. Except dead.

Mostly the older teachers were busy keeping order and worrying about not letting the kids get out of hand. Some of them were trying to *improve* everybody by telling how we could be just like them if we only had manners. And if we worked hard. And looked good.

I didn't believe them. I knew I couldn't be like them. Never. They couldn't be like me, either. They never saw the holler. They were living different lives. And even if it was true, I wouldn't care to be like them. Never loosening up to make a rhyme or a joke and laugh like Mr. McCoy, or even to sing and pray and get the Holy Spirit like Aunt Lottie.

Going to school meant suffering and trouble, yet the law said I had to go and if I stayed out too much, they blamed Aunt Lottie. The law was not fair. Some days going to school was as hard as Jesus Christ climbing Calvary Hill with the heavy cross. Every step I took in school brought pain. There were scoldings, fights, kids laughing at me, notes home, detention, and class changes. Seemed as if the City of Chicago was dishing up nothing but trouble for kids, and school was where I went to get my serving. They gave me seconds without my asking.

"I can't take time off to go talking to teachers," Aunt Lottie said. "I do that, we won't have food on the table. I just barely keep the wolf from the door now."

I worried all the time about Lizzie and just didn't know what to do. It was a terrible dilemma. Mr. McCoy taught me that word. It means trouble with no good answers. Only bad ones. It was MY word. It was me.

If I fought Lizzie and a note came home, then Aunt Lottie would be real sad. She'd take me to church all the time, thinking if I just sit there long enough I'll be raised up to the Lord in my heart.

I can't sit still very long. I don't know how come

church causes me to itch or have a running nose or cough or need to — what's the word? — *urinate*! Yes, that's the nice word. Ms. Walker says it's politer'n saying I have to go *pee*. I wonder what makes some words politer. I guess the longness of the word. If it's mighty long, it's mighty polite. Practically all the dirty words kids yell or spray-paint on walls are short. Mostly four letters. How come? I wonder. Because *love* and *aunt* and a whole bunch of good words are four letters, too. Even *good* is four letters.

Church has to be the hardest place for sitting still in the whole galaxy.

Galaxy is a gorgeous word.

I hated to get out from under the wonderful soft warm quilt, but I had to get up and wash and dress. "Live long and prosper," I told myself in the mirror as I pulled my ears into points. I would look amazingly like a Vulcan if my skin was green.

Today I was actually going to get to help prepare the birthday.

"I believe Ada could make the frosting all by herself tomorrow," Jen had said, last thing last night. I wasn't sure I had heard her right.

Aunt Lottie agreed. "She can do a fine job. She does all her chores well."

"I believe it posalutely absotively without question," Mr. McCoy said, "and it is *my* cake so I get to choose the froster. I choose Ada. Will you do it, girl?"

I bobbed my head like a balloon in the wind.

With all of them believing in me, I began to believe I could do it, too.

By the time I was downstairs opening up that heavy door that sealed off the cellar, I knew in my heart that I wouldn't be able to do anything about Lizzie or about school. I was trapped like a muskrat or a raccoon, locked in and helpless, just waiting for nothing.

Softly, I shut the door behind me. Coming down into the cellar always meant leaving those troubles behind me, the way shinnying up to the tree house Pa built for Will Junior and me used to do long ago. Otherwise, worrisome ideas kept running back into my head again and again. I couldn't stop them.

But there's no time for worrisome ideas on Washington's Birthday. It's important for a froster to keep her whole attention on the cherry frosting every single minute. And that's what I did.

Carefully, as if they were new-lain eggs, I carried the present and the card. I was dressed up in a new green plaid dress with a big white collar that Aunt Lottie had just finished sewing for me. It went nicely with my blonde hair. I felt pretty. Aunt Lottie looked fine in her rustley black church dress with the netted sleeves.

As soon as we gave Mr. McCoy his sweater,

he put it on, saying that a gray cardigan sweater was what he needed most in the world and Aunt Lottie must have been eavesdropping when he was saying his prayers for it.

"And handmade," he said, so pleased that he kissed Aunt Lottie on her cheek and made her blush. "You have golden hands, Lottie," he told her, causing her to laugh so much she shook with pleasure. "You and Jen surely keep yourselves busy with your beautiful needlework."

"Satan finds mischief for idle hands to do," Aunt Lottie answered. She enjoyed the praise but she had to protect herself from the evil eye. "So we keep our hands busy."

We all sat around the big wooden table that was covered with Jen's new filet-stitched lace cloth, and we ate praline ice cream and chocolates and drank soda pop.

Jen and Aunt Lottie talked about kinfolks back home and old times. Mr. McCoy didn't say much; he and I just listened and laughed a lot at funny happenings.

Then it was time for the cake and the singing. Last year I was a dummy, soundless and hopeless. But now I sang good and loud.

The only one louder than me was Mr. McCoy himself. I could see him breathing deeply, preparing himself.

"Happy birthday to you/me
Happy birthday to you/me
Happy birthday, George McCoy
Happy birthday to you/me!"

He bellowed it, so Jen was left holding her ears. "I have to shout to make up for all those lost birthdays," he explained. Then he leaned over and whispered to me, "You look beautiful tonight, Ada. Green is your color. If I were you, I'd never wear anything but green."

"Stop putting nonsense in the child's head," Aunt Lottie scolded, but she wasn't really mad.

"Isn't she beautiful?" he demanded. "Isn't she?"

Both women agreed that I was.

I felt beautiful. I felt like I had a real family.

Almost.

FIVE

"I've got to get ready for tomorrow," I reminded myself. "Mr. McCoy *ree*-quires my help."

That's a favorite word of mine. And this afternoon I'd picked up a new one. As I was leaving the classroom, Ms. Walker had called after me, "Hurry, Ada, don't linger so Lizzie can spot you coming out alone." She usually walked us outside, except on afternoons when she stayed to give extra help to LaVerne or some of the others. Not many kids wanted tutoring, but LaVerne always did. "Go with your group, Ada," the teacher had advised me.

Well, they weren't *my* group, but they were *a* group. I went out with them. For two weeks I'd managed to stay clear of Lizzie. That was one sharp teacher back in there, mindful of everything and doing her best to avoid trouble. *Linger* was beautiful. It meant hang out same as dawdle meant that, but it had a much better taste to it. When you dawdled, you got scolded for it. Same as when you hung out. But when you lingered — no scolding, I was sure. I could tell by the music of saying it.

Going to the grocery cabinet, I dug around in it till I came up with a Yodel aluminum foil wrapper. Aunt Lottie saved foil and plastic bags and wrappers for using again. "Waste not, want not," she always said. Lucky she waste-notted rubber bands, too. I wound the foil around the second finger of my right hand, then slipped a tiny rubber band onto it. I spread my fingers out wide in front of me. It looked neat. "Silverfinger — " I tried out how it sounded.

"Pushers and dealers better not linger,
Better beware! Here comes Silverfinger!"

Leaping from the chair I was standing on, I turned as I hit the floor, holding my bent arm close to my hip, my metal finger now the barrel of a gun. "All right all you crooks and dealers, I'm going to clean this place up right now." I pushed my chest out as if I had C cups.

"No more reefers. No more pills. No more crack!"

And because I'd heard Aunt Lottie say a million times it was cigarettes helped kill Pa, I added,

"No more smokes. No more nothing. Ratatata-tat!" I sprayed invisible enemies with invisible bullets. I waited for them to crumple onto the old green linoleum floor. Then I smiled, dusted off my hands, and set about my chores.

First I closed the brown Castro convertible that I slept on. Then I made Aunt Lottie's bumpy old bed, thinking that the white sheets always smelled so lovely and fresh. I swept the waxed floors, first with the straw broom and then with the dry mop. Aunt Lottie liked her floors to gleam and she spared no cost to always buy Johnson's Glo-Coat because she believed in it. I had to rub the floors real shiny because Aunt Lottie ran what she called a 'spection soon as she came home.

"Ada? How are you keeping, girl? 'Spection," she'd call, the moment she unlocked the door.

One thing is sure. Aunt Lottie has got to win the prize for the cleanest woman in the world. Most likely she got to be that way when she first came up from the mountains. The only jobs she could get were scrubbing other folks' houses, and washing and ironing and waxing and polishing. It must've turned her head around some. Then she got this job in a restaurant, preparing all the vegetables and stuff for the cooks. It's a lot better, but the damage was done. She had become *too clean.*

Bet she was real sloppy before, when she was living in the hills like me. Bet she didn't go 'round all the time saying, "Cleanliness is next to Godliness. Cleanliness is next to Godliness." Bet she didn't even say that one time when she was young.

She might even have picked her nose.

No! Not Aunt Lottie. She never did that.

Now she repeats "Cleanliness is next to Godliness" regular like a commercial. Only I'm not tolerated to change her channel.

The thing that seems really strange to me is how God managed to stay so clean when He had all those dirty chores to do.

When God had to create the whole world, and make Adam out of the mud down by the riverside, and then make Eve out of Adam, how did He stay spotless? That was dirty dirty work. Maybe because He is God, He can sit around shaping and stomping and handling mud and still come out shining clean. That's a pretty big miracle just by itself.

I used to spend a lot of time thinking about the stories I heard read aloud in Sunday School. I loved listening to them, but sometimes, afterward, I had trouble believing them. Now, Aunt Lottie — she believes everything that comes from the church. If Preacher or some Sister or Brother told her, "Lottie, the Lord doesn't favor your eating chocolate any more" — She loves chocolate much as I do. It's one way we know we're kin. — she'd just stop right in the middle of a first bite of a Hershey's bar or a Nestlé bar and she'd throw the rest away and never buy another chocolate bar on Friday nights when she gets paid. Never. I know Aunt Lottie.

I hope no one would ever think of saying such an awful thing to her.

Aunt Lottie's biggest enemy was dust. She was an expert on dust. She could calculate how long dust was in a place just by looking. " 'Spection — " she'd announce, soon as she came in, puffing from all those stairs, and she took off her shoes first thing and stuffed her feet into her open-toed vinyl slippers without backs. "Whee! Praise the Lord," she'd say in relief. Then — "Ada, this dust here under the chair must be paying rent. It's been living with us long enough."

"Got to move, girl," I told myself. "Do the chores fast."

First, I carefully watered all the plants, geraniums, and spiders, the gorgeous coleus and the tall rubber plant, the avocado tree and the pots of African violets, all the greenery that stretched across one side of the living room and made up Aunt Lottie's garden.

Then with a dustcloth, I brushed over the furniture quickly: chairs, table, bureau, lamp, and brass candlesticks. Living in the city needed a lot of furniture. I did everything except the TV. That I saved for last because it had to be done a special way, with love and care.

* * *

Aunt Lottie had bought it for me the second week I was in the city. She bought it "on time" she said. Mr. McCoy explained to me how that worked. The store lends it to you, and you pay a little every single week till you're all paid up and it's yours to keep — and now it's all paid up. Auntie has a printed paper in her Bible drawer that says so.

One night, a delivery man with Mr. McCoy helping him just brought this great box right up into the living room. That was when I couldn't talk. I sat there on the sofa real still and just watched.

"I bought this special for you, honey," Aunt Lottie said, her soft round face wrinkled into a big smile, the first time I saw her do that. She was pretty except for the no teeth. "I was lucky to get such a fine set secondhand." She gave the delivery man two dollars, and he lifted his hat by the peak to her. "Even secondhand it cost a pile of money. We've got to take care of it, child."

To Mr. McCoy, who had set about installing the TV, Aunt Lottie began whispering in a low voice — which I tried my best to hear. "Ain't she a sweet, pitiful little thing? Ain't said a word these two weeks, not one blessed sound. Not one *amen* in church. But she's not dumb. She can think and talk same as all of us. Just sorrowing for her Pa and for all her troubles. Just scared.

"And her Pa, my sister's one-and-only son who lived to grow to manhood, coughing from the mines and burning up with sadness for his wife and his dead child — and all the time smoking those infernal cigarettes till he burned out his lungs and the Lord took him. Leaving this mite with no Ma, no Pa, just old Aunt Lottie, who already has enough trouble doing for herself these days." She shook her head. "I do believe in the Lord, but sometimes His ways are mighty strange."

"Not so strange, Lottie," Mr. McCoy answered, untangling the silver spaghetti wires behind the large wooden box with the glass face. "You need her, and she needs you."

"Yes," Aunt Lottie sighed. "Family is always better'n no family."

"In some cases. From personal experience, I'd say sometimes no family can be better than some family."

"Uh-uh." Aunt Lottie stood firm. "Even a bad relation is better than none. A person without kin ties is like a leaf blowing around in the wind. Weightless. No one takes real notice of him, and no one misses him when he withers and drops down."

"Then you've got to choose the right kin," Mr. McCoy insisted stubbornly.

Aunt Lottie frowned, but he didn't see because he was setting up the aerial.

* * *

I fetched the special chamois cloth saved for this purpose and I set to work dusting the TV. All my friends came from inside the box: Kermit, Big Bird, Ernie and Bert, Batman and Robin, Charlie Brown and Lucy, Pinocchio, Yertle the Turtle, Peter Pan, Mr. Spock. There were dozens of them, all the funny bright characters that could never die from birthing a child, or burning up of fever, or choking from cigarettes. They would never get any sickness because they were only alive on film. They were pictures, and pictures were reliable. The cold wind can't get to pictures.

I owned a picture. It was of my mother and my father. That was how, even though I never did really see my own mother, I knew her face. My picture is a raggedy small, brown-and-white snapshot I took from Pa's shaving mirror the day of his burial, when I heard the neighbors discussing how they were going to send me up to the city to live. The picture showed Pa young with a mustache, smiling, his arm around a pretty, laughing woman, her long light hair fluffed around her thin delicate face.

Pictures are forever. You can count on them. The snapshot was in a large frame now, standing on the table right near the davenport where I sleep. Soon as Aunt Lottie saw that I'd brought that picture with me, and after she finished crying over her dead kin, she'd said, "Saturday I am going to buy us a frame. What kind of frame would you like best, Ada?"

She'd talked to me like I could talk, but I couldn't.

Saturday, she'd taken me by the hand — in the other hand she carefully carried the picture in an envelope — and we traveled all the way to Michigan Avenue to a store full of wood and glass frames of all kinds. I pointed out this one the minute I saw it because it had the big mirror border and reminded me of Pa's shaving mirror where the picture came from. Also, I could see myself while I looked at the picture, and I could see if I looked like them. I think I'm getting to look like my mother. Maybe if I'm lucky.

Aunt Lottie turned out to be real nice, though she is strict. I did want to listen to her and do her bidding, but it was just too hard. Aunt Lottie mentioned at least once every night that school was my beholden duty. I did try to go, but staying home was so much nicer and easier and safer.

Sometimes after a bad fight when I got my face bloodied or my knees scraped badly, Aunt Lottie herself would keep me home, locked safely in the empty apartment all day. Double-locked. The locks were protection. There was no protection at all in the streets.

And I had the television for company.

Once I pulled the shades in the living room, it was dark and peaceful and quiet, the only light being the light of the tube like a lantern glimmering in a long safe tunnel. Anyway, TV was fun and I was learning from it, more than I ever learned going to school. The baby programs — which no one outside could ever know I watched — practiced numbers and easy words. I always repeated after the teacher and did all the exercises, and I made all the drawings whenever the TV people said I should. I could do most things fine.

Doing the chores didn't bother me a bit. I used to take care of things for Pa back home the same way. Except not so fussy. I wanted to do things for Aunt Lottie. When she came home nights, her feet were so tired she could hardly stand, the veins bulging like jump ropes.

Today I would have everything finished before my afternoon programs because I was going to try to do homework afterward.

Homework!

Ms. Walker had thought about something so interesting to talk about in class that I stayed awake all day, even though last night, after Aunt Lottie was snoring, I turned the TV back on and watched *Goldfinger* on the late-night movie.

In the morning, to avoid Lizzie I snuck into school early, so early that only Ms. Walker was in the room. She was standing by the window looking out and drinking hot tea and eating a chocolate chip cookie.

"Good morning, Ada." She seemed glad to see me even if it was before the bell.

"Morning, Ms. Walker."

"I was about to wash the boards," she said.

I saw the basin of water and the orange sponge on some newspapers up on her desk.

"Would you like to help, Ada?"

"Sure. I'll do it all."

I took the sponge and squeezed it out but not too dry, and began working, even strokes up and down with lots of rinses for the sponge so the boards wouldn't come out all streaky.

I dumped the basin of dirty water in the janitor's sink in the hall, and rinsed the sponge and brought all the stuff back to my teacher.

"Thank you. What a thorough job you did, Ada." Ms. Walker looked around at the boards. "They haven't looked that clean since school started. Here — have some cookies." She took out a sack of the extra-chocolaty kind — with walnuts — from her top desk drawer.

I wanted one, but I wanted to be polite. So I didn't take. I put my hands behind my back.

"Don't you like this kind? Take a few," Ms. Walker urged me.

Gladly, I reached in and took three. "Thank you," I said. "I love chocolate chip cookies. They're my favorite."

"Mine, too," the teacher said, sealing the sack and putting it away. "You wouldn't care to be board monitor, would you, Ada? It would mean coming in early every morning."

My mouth was full of cookie sweetness, and my heart was full of sweetness, too. I just nodded my head hard.

"Fine," she said.

I headed for my seat. I was happy.

"While you're waiting," Ms. Walker said, "why don't you pick up a book from the library shelf and look at it?"

"Can't read," I said. All my happiness was gone.

"Well, then — you might take one and look at the pictures. There's an interesting new book right on top of the bookcase, with pictures of the first drawings done by cavemen on the walls of their caves. The first human writing, really."

I didn't budge. I just sat there and finished chewing the cookies without tasting the sweetness any more. Why did *reading* always have to be *so* important?

Ms. Walker got busy setting out the work supplies for the day in three separate piles: alphabet charts, tracing paper, and lined composition paper.

When the other kids came, she began the lesson by telling how the very first writing was pictures scratched on stone and drawings on the walls of caves. She passed around this big book with the cavemen's drawings, telling us they were found deep inside a dark cave in the mountains between France and Spain, and they were still there to see. I couldn't believe how good the artists were. Some of their drawings of animals were beautiful. There wasn't time to look through and see every picture. The book was big. I was real sorry that I didn't look before the others came.

Then Ms. Walker pointed to the wall alphabet chart while each of us pointed to her own desk chart, and together we said the letters one by one, tracing them over carefully, over and over and over. As soon as someone thought she had a letter — both the sound and the shape — she tried to write it on her good white paper to hand in.

I felt two ways about doing all this. It was baby work, not real sixth-grade work, and I was already eleven years old. I knew that sometimes I could do all this just fine, and other times I couldn't. It didn't hurt to try now, I supposed, and I decided to stay awake and stay with it. If it turned out nice, I'd hand the paper in. If not, I'd just crumple it up.

"Homework for tonight," Ms. Walker said briskly as she finished the lesson. "Write the alphabet. Capitals. As nicely as you can. And, for extra credit — that means nobody *has* to do this unless she's dying to — write the alphabet in small letters. You may take your desk chart home overnight so you can have a model to work from."

I studied my chart. The letters, the big ones and the little ones, were clear today and attached to sounds. They had meanings. To be sure I was doing it right, I showed the ones I wrote in class to LaVerne, who sat near me. LaVerne said mine looked perfect to her. At the end of the lesson, just before sewing period, I turned in my paper. First paper I ever did in that school, so I made up my mind I might as well do the homework, too.

The alphabet chart that Ms. Walker had sent us home with was, this minute, lying on the kitchen table.

But that was for later, much much later.

Once the shades were drawn tight, I flipped on the TV set and sat down on the floor, close, waiting for the pictures on the screen. There they were.

> "Sunny day, sweepin' the clouds away,
>   On my way to where the air is sweet
>   Can you tell me how to get —
>   How to get to Sesame Street?
> "Come and play, everything's A-OK . . ."

I sang along with them, and then I leaned back on my elbow and watched them begin to fool around. Bob and Linda and Gordon. Kermit. Luis. Big Bird and Elmo. Not once did I itch or have to blow my nose or urinate. Not once during the whole hour. I counted with the Count and the happy little twiddlebugs. I practiced the letter Z again and again. I laughed at Miami Mice.

I could've lived my whole life on *Sesame Street.* The only thing that might have made it even more fun was if someone else were there watching with me to laugh along, and to repeat some of the jokes to.

But if someone else were there, she might interrupt the program the way Aunt Lottie did all the time, so I was better off alone.

Still, a kid just my age who kept quiet would have been fun. Or a real little kid, two or three years old, who I could explain things to and cuddle.

I wasn't about to complain. Aunt Lottie was always saying that a person couldn't have everything.

Watching TV, I forgot that I didn't have everything. Mostly, I sat hugging my knees, my eyes fixed on the screen. I really felt I was on *Sesame Street.* I knew all those puppets and the people there better than almost anyone in my life. And none of them could hurt me. Or wanted to hurt me — or anyone. How could Kermit or Big Bird be an enemy?

Afterward, there was *Mr. Rogers' Neighborhood.* A real baby program. Lizzie and her friends would drop dead with joy if they knew that tough Ada Garland, me, watched Mr. Rogers. But I did because he was such a kind man. He reminded me a little of my Pa.

When Pa was younger — when he took that picture that we had in the mirror frame — he was much bigger and stronger than Mr. Rogers. But Pa was patient with us kids, and friendly with folks, and he liked animals. Pa could fight if he had to, but he never went out looking for it.

That was what he taught me and Will Junior. "Don't go looking for trouble, but if trouble comes seeking you out with its fists, you better be ready." And he taught us how to take care of ourselves. I was a good fighter because of Pa's training, and I didn't go looking for trouble. I swear I didn't. But trouble came looking for me.

Now this Mr. Rogers, he wouldn't be able to fight a paper doll. I loved to listen to the easy way he sang looking right at me.

> *"I'm taking care of you*
> *Taking good care of you*
> *For once I was very little, too*
> *Now I take care of you."*

When *Mr. Rogers' Neighborhood* was over, I flipped the dial to *Popeye* or *Yogi Bear* or *Little House on the Prairie.* There were enough wonderful programs so I didn't have to move off the floor for hours, and I didn't even hear the lock

71

turn or the door open or Aunt Lottie call, "Ada? 'Spection time."

She came on in, and I ran and got her house-slippers for her. "A crook could come in and steal every little thing we own, and you wouldn't take any notice if you're watching TV," she fretted.

"Couldn't steal the TV," I said. "I'd notice that."

Aunt Lottie tapped my head as I helped her with her shoes. "That machine got you hypno-tized. It'd be better if you found some nice friends to visit with. Some nice girlfriends."

"I don't need girlfriends." I switched off the set and went to unpack the bag of food Aunt Lottie had carried in. "Kentucky Fried," I recognized. "That smells real good. Like home."

"My feet are too tired to hold up for cooking tonight," Aunt Lottie explained. "You know I like to make my own home-fried chicken. But this has to be good enough."

"Yours is better," I said, and it was the truth, "but this is okay."

We ate our dinner, and then I washed up and took the trash downstairs. Aunt Lottie said I'd done a real good job of cleaning that day. She couldn't find a speck of dust. Finally, I sat down at the kitchen table with my composition paper and a pencil Auntie had whittled to a dangerous point with her kitchen knife.

I studied the model first, saying it out loud: "A — A — A — A." When I thought I had it firmly in my mind, I tried to draw an exact copy of it onto the page. Twice, the pencil slipped. I couldn't bear to erase because the eraser left red marks. I crumpled up the whole sheet and threw it away and began again. I took the greatest care that each letter should have a little extra wiggle or tail for decoration.

Aunt Lottie, sitting on the other side of the table, crocheting, looked over at me from time to time but didn't say anything. She just seemed sort of pleased, her cheeks puffed out a little.

When I'd been working for a very long time, she stood up and shuffled over behind me, looking at my page of letters.

"Ada, you write a nice hand, big clear letters like your Pa and your brother. I didn't know you could do that."

"Are all the letters facing the right way?" I asked. I couldn't tell. They always looked right to me.

Aunt Lottie really studied the page, her finger pointing to each letter in turn and checking it against the chart. "Far as I can tell, it's perfect." She patted my shoulder, and I felt that pat clear down to my toes like an electric shock.

I wanted to turn around and hug Aunt Lottie and bawl, but I just couldn't. I just couldn't. So I kept staring at the letters, the truly beautiful letters that I'd managed to put in rows on that clean page.

SIX

"Don't need no zinc ointment —
For my special appointment."

I tried it out in my head as I locked the door,
but it wasn't a good rhyme. Will Junior used to
say a true rhyme:

"Makes sense, sounds good
Can be clearly understood."

Ointment didn't make sense. The problem was
I didn't have any other word to rhyme with *appointment.* Another hard word was orange. Once
I tried to think of a rhyme for *orange* and it nearly
drove me crazy for an hour. I was watching a *Star
Trek* rerun, and all I could think of was *orange,
orange, orange.* After the program I didn't know

what I'd watched, and I had no rhyme.

Appointment was Mr. McCoy's word. Last night he'd called up to me as I was carrying the garbage out after supper — Aunt Lottie doesn't tolerate the garbage to linger in the pail overnight — "Can I make an appointment with you, Ada, for tomorrow? We need to get the newspapers ready for Billy-boy."

"Sure," I agreed.

"Roger." Mr. McCoy raised his hand and he made a tiny circle with his thumb and first finger. That meant okay. *Roger* was the way English people in England said okay. Pretty weird to use a boy's name that way, but I liked it when Mr. McCoy said it. It reminded me of the old war movies they have on sometimes late at night.

"Bomb Berlin."

"Roger. Over."

And the handsome pilot flies off way into the clouds.

Whenever anyone in the building threw out old newspapers, Mr. McCoy collected them and saved them in stacks in the basement. Once a month, he tied them up in twenty-five-pound bundles and sold them to Billy-boy, who came in his bright blue van to get them. Billy-boy was strange, a full-grown man who didn't ever have to shave, Mr. McCoy said, because he had something wrong with him inside.

At first, I didn't see any sense in anyone coming

to buy old newspapers, but Mr. McCoy explained that Billy carried them back to a recycling factory where they got turned right back into some kind of clean paper, maybe not newspaper but some kind of paper. Prob'ly toilet paper.

"Recycling sounds like bicycling," I said.

"Does," Mr. McCoy agreed. "Must have something to do with going round and round and never getting used up."

I still couldn't figure it. I never saw toilet paper with printing on it (though there is some with fancy designs) except back home where some folks use strips of newspaper in their outhouses.

"Chemistry," Mr. McCoy said. "Science!" And he snapped his fingers sharp. "Scientists can do most anything they want to nowadays, Ada. You go to school regular and pay attention, and you might get to do some big science things, too. Real big."

"Can they turn water into wine?"

"Nope. That's one thing they can't do yet. But I betcha someone's working on it. Maybe one of my relatives." And he had a funny smile on his face.

"Don't say anything about that to Aunt Lottie," I warned. "She's always grumbling about men playing God. It'll get her mad."

"I've already erased it from my mind."

I pushed against our door a couple of times to be sure it was locked, and then I unwrapped the aluminum foil from my gun finger. Mr. McCoy always said when I pressed that same finger on a string so he could fasten a knot, it was stronger than any other knots he ever made. "You're a big help, Ada," he'd say.

Whenever he tied up the papers, he separated out a good picture magazine for me. Today there was a practically new-looking one with a picture of Madonna on the cover. "That's *Rolling Stone* magazine," he said. "Mostly pictures of musicians. But Jen saved you one, too. Jen — " he called. "Ada's here. Bring the church magazine for her."

Out came Jen, out of her bright white kitchen into the working part of the basement, and she brought me a thin glossy magazine with a beautiful small flowering tree on its cover, all the white blossoms open in the sunshine. "Recognize that?" she asked.

"Dogwood. Last one I saw was down home."

"Did you know dogwood has a story 'tached to it? A real sad story. My own grandma told it to me when I was small."

I love stories. "Will you tell it to me, Jen?" She had a sweet soft voice, so I moved up close to her to be sure to hear every word.

"Well, Grandma said the dogwood was once a giant-sized tree with real bright-colored blossoms. It grew in many places in the world, including the Holy Land. A tall dogwood tree cut

77

in two was what they made the cross out of that Jesus carried on Calvary, and they crucified Him on it.

"After that, the dogwood tree never grew tall again. The flowers faded and changed their shape so they're sort of cross-shaped, and if you look underneath a flower you see those rust-colored marks that stand for the nails they hammered into His hands and His feet."

"That *is* sad, Jen."

"It's what they call a legend," Mr. McCoy added. "There's no proof."

"I'll thank you to stay out of this, Doubting Thomas," Jen said in a scolding way.

"The name's George," he said, smiling to get back in her good favor. "I believe it, but it is a legend. We can't prove it."

"Thanks for the picture. I love it," I said.

"Visit with us, Jen, while we tie the papers," Mr. McCoy said. That was a pretty strange invite. Mostly Jen was so busy cleaning or cooking or sewing she had no time to waste outside the apartment. But this afternoon she went in and fetched her crocheting, and then she sat down on the old leather hassock near the newspaper bin.

Mr. McCoy lifted a batch of newspapers onto his big, flat scale. He added some more then, poking their edges into a straight row. "Say, Ada, you were in a fight the other day, weren't you?"

I didn't answer.

"I could tell," he said. "I could smell it. I just let it lay when you fibbed, but I could tell."

"Sorry," I murmured. I didn't like to lie.

He looked dead at me. "Ada, you ever wonder why I don't talk about my kin none? The way Jen goes on about hers all the time and Lottie, too, going back all the way, telling tales of family. Grandmothers and grandfathers and the whole lot. Didn't you ever wonder that I have no grandfathers to talk about?" Picking up the spool of string, he began to wind the string round and round the stack of papers, crossing it over for strength.

I was uncomfortable because I *had* wondered, and all sorts of crazy ideas *had* come into my head. "I just figured you didn't do that kind of talking. Maybe Jen didn't like you to — "

"You're right," Jen said sharply.

"Girl, you are smart," Mr. McCoy said. "Jen doesn't like me to bring them up, but today I'm going to make an exception."

I moved over to hold my finger on the string-crossing place as he pulled it into a tight knot.

"Ada, I come from a family of fighters and murderers."

"Murderers?" I giggled. Mr. McCoy's kin? "How could that be? You remind me of Fred Rogers on TV. Mr. Rogers. You couldn't hurt anyone. Nor your brothers nor your family."

"Not my 'mediate family, Ada. Not my brothers or sister or Ma or Pa. But go back a little. My granduncles and my grandpa and cousins and all them were terrible fighters. They were a *dis-grace*."

Jen made an agreeing noise.

"What did they fight over?"

"No one really knows. That's the thing about fights. Afterward, people can't usually say why they started. There are a lot of different stories about my kin — in books."

"They wrote about *your family* in books?" I was really impressed.

"Not nice stories, Ada," Jen said, working her needle busily. "Not stories to be proud of."

"Much as I understand it," Mr. McCoy went on, "just after the Civil War — that was the war between the states that wanted to keep black folks as slaves and the other states that said no — a man named Anse Hatfield on the slave side hid out and shot Harmon McCoy, who fought on the other side. That happened well over a hundred years ago."

"Well, that was a war," I said. "They were soldiers."

"This was after the war was settled. The Hat-fields lived in Logan County, West Virginia. My folks farmed just a little ways off in Pike County, Kentucky. The two families were living real close on the Tug Fork River. Well, the McCoys never forgot Harmon. They wanted revenge. They bided their time.

"A few years after, a Hatfield and a McCoy got into an argument about who owned a hog that was running free on the mountainside. The owner was supposed to cut a mark on the hog's ear so he'd know his own, but this mark wasn't clear. Both claimed the hog. They squabbled and squabbled and finally took it to court. The Hatfields won, and that's when real trouble started.

"Hatfield and McCoy men began shooting at one another. Ada, they were murdering one another. Gunning each other down."

"In the woods, in the bushes, on the river. Everywhere," Jen said sadly. "Murdering each other."

"Then — as it had to happen — a McCoy girl, Rose Anne, fell in love with Jahnse Hatfield. He carried her off, but his Pa wouldn't let him marry her. They sent her back, and she died soon after that of a broken heart."

That part really was sad. I could feel for Rose Anne. "Did she really die of a broken heart?"

"Yup. She was a pretty little thing. Just pined away. So my kin got even angrier.

"Well — they kept at it — men murdering each other and even killing women. For years and years. It finally simmered down, and then it died out. It never settled anything. I don't take any pride in them, Ada. That's why I don't talk about them.

"Back when I met Jen, she wouldn't look at a McCoy. Her folks were church people. Law abiding. Then I wore her down, but she wouldn't marry me lest I promised her I wouldn't go boasting or talking about the McCoys. And I kept my promise to this very day."

"He kept the promise," Jen said. "And I took the name McCoy. At the beginning it was hard. Most times when new folks heard my name, they made jokes about feuding and killing. 'Where d'ya hide the shotgun?' someone'd ask. Or, 'Wiped out any Hatfields lately?' It's embarrassing, Ada, to carry a bad name. There's nothing to be done about ours anymore. But when George said you were hurt again fighting the other day, I said, 'Time to talk about our family disgrace to Ada. Time to tell her where the McCoy hot blood and their fighting got them. All that hurting and bleeding. This world is hard enough. We don't need to add to its troubles.' "

It wasn't fair that those people put down Jen. She didn't hold with roughness. She never deserved it. "I don't look for fights," I said. "They seem to look for me. I didn't start that one the other day. Honest." There were tears in my eyes.

"I believe you," Jen said, giving me a handkerchief. "But you have to look for ways to get out of fighting. You have to do your best to 'void it."

"That's being a coward."

"No. That's being smart," they said together one-time like twins.

"We're starting to talk together," Jen said, smiling.

"Ada, if it's life or death — like with a dealer — and you have to fight, then do it. Otherwise, look for another way out," Mr. McCoy said. "Promise you'll try."

"I'll try," I said. "I really will."

Jen came and lifted the hair covering my scarred cheek and she kissed me on the scratches. "Lottie will be so glad," she said.

"She knows I had a fight?"

They nodded.

I was surprised. These old people with their bad eyes sure saw a bunch of things. Aunt Lottie knew and had kept quiet!

"We're going on a class trip next month to the zoo," I told them. "The whole class is going — except fighters."

"That's good news." Mr. McCoy was pleased. "That's a reason to stay peaceable. And when you get to the zoo, please say hello to the hyena for me."

"The hyena?"

"Yeah. He's an animal no one favors. God didn't make him beautiful or brave or even sweet-smelling. But he just goes right on living and laughing, and he pays no mind to the rest of the world."

"I'll look out for him," I promised. I never met a laughing animal. Cats don't. Dogs don't. Squirrels don't or raccoons. I was curious.

"Now let's get these papers done," Mr. McCoy said. "Billy-boy is due any time now, and you know he can't wait. He has no understanding, so he gets real cranky like a baby."

We worked faster, and I thought some more about the strangeness of Billy-boy. He really was a ree-tard (Mr. McCoy said that was how you say it), a short heavy young man with brown hair and a pasty-white skin covered all over with freckles, who could drive a van but who couldn't hardly talk. He had brown eyes that were round and shiny and stared like marbles.

Mr. McCoy said that Billy-boy could never think of things to say the way other people did. Nothing came into his head. That's why he was so quiet. He wasn't a bad fellow. Just not smart. He worked hard on his van keeping it spotless, and he was always most polite to Mr. McCoy and wouldn't let him do any heavy picking up or loading.

Because I was sitting every day now in Ms. Walker's special class, I decided to pay particular attention to Billy-boy this time. I would really study how he was.

I was thinking about all the girls in my class who already had quiet, staring ways like he had. When they grew up, maybe they'd be like him. And what about me when I got big? If I stayed in Ms. Walker's class?

"Herro," Billy-boy said, soon as he arrived. He didn't say things exactly right. He smiled a big fat smile like he was on a Crest commercial. And he kept that smile on his face too long.

"Twenty bundles," Mr. McCoy said. He took a paper and figured it all right out, then signed his name and gave the paper to Billy-boy. A check would come in the mail next week from Billy-boy's father who owned the recycling factory.

"How you keeping, Billy-boy?" Mr. McCoy asked.

Billy-boy grinned. He was always happy except when he was kept waiting. "Good," he said and he carried out two bundles by the strings as if they were weightless. He was very strong.

"You met my assistant?" Mr. McCoy asked him next trip.

He gave us the big smile again, but his eyes were far away, someplace else. "Mmmm," he said, and then again, "Mmmm."

"My helper. This young lady. Miss Ada."

"*Ms.* Ada," I corrected him.

"Ms. Ada."

Billy-boy dipped his head in my direction but he wasn't really paying attention to me.

When he finished carrying all the papers out, and Mr. McCoy checked to see that he had the slip safely stored in his pocket, he left. And after he drove off, Mr. McCoy said, "There's something to be learned here, Ada. If Billy'd been born to poor folks, he'd be locked up somewheres, or he'd be living on the streets. He wouldn't be clean and nice doing a regular job like the rest of us. They'd probably keep him in a hospital that was run tight as a jail almost."

"Why's that? He wouldn't do anything bad."

"Because he can't take care of himself. His mind works too slow. He can't read or write at all. They had to teach him to dress himself over and over before he could finally learn. Even buttoning a shirt in the right buttonholes was hard for him. Till this very day he can't tie his own shoelaces. See, he always wears loafers."

I looked down at my own loafers, and he caught on to what I was thinking.

"But you wear sneakers, too, and you can tie them just fine when you've a mind to." He meant mostly I keep them dangling for style. "Billy can't. Lucky for him his father has this paper factory and plenty of money, so Billy got a chance. Just plain lucky."

"He wasn't so lucky to get born like that."

"You got a point. But who gets to choose the way they're born? Point is, Billy got a chance to live like a human being. That's all that's needed.

That chance. Some get it by who they're born to or where they're born, and some got to make it for themselves."

"You talking about me, Mr. McCoy?"

"About us all. Human beings."

I had the feeling it was mostly about me, and I also had the feeling it was mostly about not fighting. Mr. McCoy was going along a side road, but I could tell where he was headed.

"Anyway, depends on what a person does with what he's got. Billy's doing what he can with the little that was given him."

I could see that.

Mr. McCoy gave me a quarter for helping with the newspaper bundling. "Go get yourself a candy bar," he said. "And, Ada, I don't need to ask you not to repeat what I told you about my family, do I?"

"I'll never tell, Mr. McCoy. Never."

"I know. Jen and I knew we could trust you. It's our secret."

"Forever," I promised and ran off to buy me a Milky Way bar. Who would have thought that about Mr. McCoy's family? I wondered if Fred Rogers had some terrible family secrets like that. Maybe that's why he's always talking about *good neighbors*. I guess you can't ever tell.

SEVEN

Either Lizzie was sick or she was playing hooky and hanging out someplace else.

I moved swiftly out of the school building just as I had these last few weeks. I chose my leaving time carefully and once I was clear of the schoolyard, I made my way speedy as 007 to my lonely upstairs hideout. I cut corners and found shortcuts through alleys, and sometimes I even doubled back to fool anyone following me.

I wished I had some special spy equipment, but I managed okay without it. Still, a wristwatch that gives all kinds of weather information and picks up radio broadcasts — or a sports car that turns into a boat if it happens to fall in Lake Michigan — would have been great.

But I was traveling in my own red sneakers, one of which had a flapping sole. I had not worn my loafers since Mr. McCoy told me why Billy-boy wore his. I was doing okay.

No sign of the enemy anywhere. I crossed my fingers.

I thought it was most likely that Lizzie was sick. Maybe it was drugs, or maybe she had a disease and was going to die. Yes, she was going to pass on. The cold cold wind had found Lizzie. "An untimely calling to the Great Beyond," Preacher always liked to say at young peoples' funerals. Well, Preacher was wrong. Any time was timely for Lizzie far as I was concerned. Soon, soon, soon. Maybe she had even passed on yesterday or last week. Or before that.

Naah. We would've heard in school.

Wonder what she's got.

I had a growing list of desirable ailments to wish on enemies. It included itches, fever, breathing sickness, fleas, asthma, hives, lice, acid stomach, warts, postnasal drip, bee bites, and muscular dystrophy. I learned that one from Jerry Lewis. The ones that sounded the worst were my favorites. Postnasal drip won the prize.

Lizzie must have been suffering from one or two of these, at least, to keep her out of school. Maybe three or four? Maybe all? Wouldn't that be lucky for me?

Wonderfully clear hospital-bed scenes in living color filled my head these days as I snuck around and hid, and waited my chance to race through the dirty streets. I came to prize the trash cans stacked out all over the sidewalks, forming pyramids of metal to hide behind. Seemed as if there were no end to the amount of garbage around. The mountains of stuffed black plastic bags helped, too.

And while I waited, I saw Lizzie, in my mind, laid out flat on her back with an arm (or arms) and a leg (or both legs) broken; Lizzie crumpled over, falling; Lizzie bleeding onto white bed sheets, and a big nurse, who looked exactly like Mrs. O'Neill, the assistant principal with the knockers, saying, "Now you've got to pay to clean these white sheets, Lizzie. Blood don't wash out"; Lizzie being fished frozen out of the lake; Lizzie holding her chest and making rattling noises when she breathed, like Pa. That could really be because Lizzie smoked a lot. She used to stand around in the schoolyard, blowing smoke where the teachers could see. She was always daring the teachers. Now, in my mind, she was gasping like a hooked fish. Gasp, Lizzie, gasp.

The doctor in charge was sometimes a handsome young one from an afternoon TV story: *General Hospital* or *One Life to Live*, but mostly it was Dr. McCoy of the Enterprise. Because I loved his name and he wore such a classy uniform. McCoy was always looking very sad as he told me the news.

"The patient requires a blood transfusion, and you are the only one in the whole world with the right blood type."

I answer him. I look a lot like Lieutenant Uhura, and my voice is sexy like hers. "I would be glad to give my blood for a small child who requires it, Dr. McCoy. Or for a blind old woman. You can take as much as you require. Why, I would be glad to linger on here just to do that. But I will never tolerate mixing my blood with evil Klingon blood like Lizzie's. Never."

Grimly, McCoy nods. He understands.

In slow motion, I turn on my stiletto heels and I go. I don't just go. I dee-part.

But once in a while, I had to come up out of these dreams and tell myself the truth.

Lizzie prob'ly isn't sick at all.

Lizzie prob'ly isn't going to die. Aunt Lottie says the good die young — like Ma and Pa and Will Junior — and Lizzie is no good. Lizzie is probably out there waiting for me this very minute. And there is no way I can get out of fighting her.

I prayed. *Lord — I am so sorry I had trouble sitting still in Your House so I didn't get myself properly saved — if Lizzie is looking for me, let her find me AFTER the trip to the zoo. You do that, Lord, for me, and I won't fidget or itch or have to go pee — urinate — in Your House ever again as long as I live. Amen!*

91

I dashed into school early every morning to wash the boards. Then, in the time that was left before the bell, Ms. Walker gave me a reading lesson, only it was mostly a talking lesson all about Pa and Will Junior and Aunt Lottie and the McCoys (but I never breathed one word about the murderers!). Sometimes I told Ms. Walker a story I thought up, and sometimes she told me a story right back.

Each day she'd show me some pages in a book. There were times when I could read the words easy. There were other days when the letters remained shapes on a page. Like I couldn't make a connection with them.

"We all have good learning days and bad ones, Ada," Ms. Walker said, and she wasn't a bit impatient or angry. "You just go at a different speed. You're coming along fine."

She was real interested the day I told her how Will Junior taught me to make rhymes, and I liked doing it. I told her about *orange* and *ointment*, and she agreed they were impossible words.

"Try putting them in the middle of the line when you're making up your verses," she said. "Put easier-rhyming words on the end." She offered me the box of fudge-stripes. "Soon you'll be able to write your poems down and then read them back to yourself — or your family — whenever you want to," she promised.

I could hardly believe that.

I was mighty glad that Ms. Walker ended reading lessons with cookies. It made learning tasty.

But life wasn't all that easy the rest of the days after the nice mornings. When somebody pushed into the line in front of me, or called me *hillbilly,* or made fun of my dress or raggedy coat, right off I was ready to punch them. I held back because of the McCoys. They trusted me. They trusted me so much, they told me a story they'd never told *anyone* else. Me, Ada Garland, they trusted. I kept my fists balled tight to my belly, and I didn't punch out when kids treated me bad. It wasn't easy at all.

In class we began to talk about the animals we would see in the zoo. We learned to spell their names and we looked at colored slides and began to draw each animal. The lions and tigers and zebras were beautiful, and the giraffes were very strange, but the hyena — Mr. McCoy was right about him — wasn't nice at all. Looking at the picture of that funny-looking critter, it was hard for me to believe he ever laughed. He didn't look as if he could or would want to. I was really dying to see him and hear for myself.

Ms. Walker was teaching us some interesting facts about the animals we would see. She said she wanted us to try to find things out for ourselves and not to believe in myths and legends. Myths and legends were interesting old stories that weren't true, but folks sometimes believed them. I remembered that when Mr. McCoy said Jen's dogwood story was a legend, Jen got mad. I didn't understand why because it was such a beautiful story, true or made up.

Ms. Walker offered us an example of something many folks believe is true: A bull gets mad when he sees something red. That started a whopper of an argument in class because the kids did believe it, and Ms. Walker said no, bulls are color-blind. When the fighter waves the red tablecloth around, it's the motion of the cloth that makes the bull mad, not the color. "Most likely a bull-fighter could wave a blue cloth or a polka-dotted cloth — any color" — Ms. Walker said — "and the bull would go for him."

LaVerne said, like she really knew, that the teacher was right. "My mother and father saw a bullfight in Mexico and they say it's moving the cloth does it."

"What were your folks doing in Mexico?" Jessica asked. Maybe she didn't believe LaVerne.

"Honeymooning."

That brought out a lot of silly noises because it meant sex.

"It was a long time ago," LaVerne said, blushing.

A lot of things Ms. Walker taught us seemed strange. During one whole lesson, Jessica, in a pink leotard top to show her B cups, and Yolanda, kept whispering loud that the teacher didn't know what she was talking about. I really wanted to punch them both. I sat on my hands.

Ms. Walker said the Lincoln Park Zoo had a Great Ape House with twenty-three gorillas in it. *Twenty-three!* She started to talk about gorillas. She said they were peaceable animals unless you pestered them a lot and they were vegetarians besides — she wrote VEGETARIANS on the board so we could all see the VEG part of it, same as in vegetable, and understand that they wouldn't eat meat — and how gorillas lived in families, and the father gorilla took care of his family.

Jessica began to laugh so loud, Ms. Walker stopped talking. "What is it, Jessica? What's so funny?"

"What you said." Jessica was choking with laughs. "How about Kong? King Kong? You know he wasn't so peaceful. He didn't live with no family of his own just eating greens. He went after a woman and carried her clear to the top of the Umpire State Building in New York City."

All around her, kids laughed.

"Empire State Building," Mrs. Walker said.

I raised my hand. "That's not a true story," I said. "That's just a made-up movie story."

"Appalachee Ada, who you telling something to?" Jessica turned mean. She didn't like anyone to disagree with her.

I wasn't scared. "It's not a myth or a legend yet," I said, "because it's not an *old* enough story."

Jessica made as if to get up and move at me. Ms. Walker asked her, "Would you like to wait in the library till this lesson is over, Jessica?"

"No, ma'am."

"But you don't seem interested in the subject."

"Oh, I'm interested, teacher — "

"Ms. Walker."

"I'm interested, *Ms. Walker.* It just sounds funny. All that talk about bulls and gorillas."

Since Yolanda was Jessica's shadow, she had to butt in. "Last night I told my uncle what you said about how elephants forget just like everyone else. You know what he said? My uncle said, 'Never you mind what that black teacher told you. Elephants got the greatest living memories of any living creatures.' He said an elephant never forgets nothing. My uncle said that and he never lies."

"Did you check out where your white uncle got his information?"

"Why you calling him my white uncle?"

"He called me your black teacher. We don't need the colors at all, do we? We know who we're talking about. So, how many elephants does your uncle know personally?"

We all loved that, all except Yolanda. Her voice went real high and screechy. "He doesn't know any elephants personally. He runs a big grocery store over on Woodlawn."

"And my mother said elephants live to be very old — like hundreds of years old — " Jessica came back into it. "She said you mean well, but you got it all mixed up. I told her you said about seventy-five is how old most elephants live till."

"Your mother's wrong in this case, Jessica."

"You saying my mother's a liar?"

"Jessica, your mother's information is not correct. I'll lend you a book to take home and show her."

Jessica poked her mouth out. "There's lies in books, too, you know."

I felt bad for Ms. Walker. Almost nobody believed her. But why should she lie to us? It was hard to credit some of the things she said because all around everyone else was saying exactly the opposite was true. Myths were everywhere.

The teacher didn't push it. "All right," she said, smiling like she didn't mind a bit that she hadn't won, "as soon as I meet a hundred-fifty-year-old elephant who remembers back to when he was a baby, I'll change my opinion. Not till then."

The subject was dropped.

The best way was to see for ourselves.

The great day was almost here.

Tomorrow.

I had to get home to do the chores and then iron my white-and-blue-checked blouse and mend the heel of my blue sock for tomorrow. And polish my loafers which I had taken to wearing again. One day Ms. Ames, our student teacher, came wearing shiny black loafers, so I knew they weren't only for retards.

I was hurrying along Forty-seventh Street, just turning a corner by an empty building, when I heard the call.

"Hi, Ada!"

It came from across the way. Looking over, I saw LaVerne, her arms filled with packages, walking with a small pretty woman, all dressed up fine.

Her mother, I knew. Her mother who once saw a bullfight with her father on their honeymoon in Mexico. Lucky LaVerne.

I stood smiling at them across the way. Then I heard the voice behind me.

"Yo. Ada."

I didn't turn.

"Yo. Ree-tart." The voice was phony sweet, mocking LaVerne's real sweet tone. The voice had more to say. "I heard your aunt's one, too — a ree-tart. And your mother was one. And your father and your brother — "

Go home, the voice of common sense told me. *Run. Don't listen. Tomorrow's the trip to the zoo. Don't pay her any mind.*

My feet were magnets locked into place.

"Ree-tart! Ree-tart! Your whole family's ree-tarts."

I looked across the street quick and saw

LaVerne walking slower behind her mother. I knew she saw Lizzie. Then her mother called for her to hurry and catch up, they were crossing over, and she did hurry, but she was still looking back. They went round the corner.

It couldn't have been worse. I had to fight, and someone in my own class knew about it. LaVerne would carry the story in tomorrow to Ms. Walker. Even if I could win, I'd lose.

"Ree-tart. Ree-tart!"

Stupid Lizzie didn't even know how to say it right.

I couldn't bear to listen anymore. I turned back to the steps where she was standing. She wasn't wearing her white jacket. She was leaning with one elbow on the iron railing, her lip out fat with hate for me.

I went right for her. I wasn't afraid, only sad. My whole life was run by outside things, and I couldn't stop them: everyone in my family dying, me not being able to read and write like others, my breasts refusing to grow, and now my trip to the zoo lost.

Why did Lizzie have to meet up with me just the very day before?

Why?

Let Mr. McCoy talk all he liked about a person trying to use what he had — like Billy-boy — and there'd always be a chance for that person. It just wasn't so. Some persons never get a real chance at anything. No matter what they try, nothing works. Like me. I'm one of those hopeless persons. A loser.

For the first time I sort of had the sunk feeling, the terrible understanding of how come the addicts came to be sticking needles in their arms.

I surprised Lizzie. I grabbed for her collar tips from both sides and gathered the cloth points tight tight together, choking her as I pulled her down off the steps so we were face to face. 'Cept her face was a little higher. I did my best to tighten my grip on the collar and bend her down.

Lizzie's hands scrambled to free her neck. She dug her long painted fingernails into my hands, and she ripped at the skin and gouged into my fingers trying to free herself.

I held on long as I could, but finally I had to let go. Lizzie began to hit at my chest, pounding away, fat fists sure of where to land to hurt the most. The first few punches were so powerful that they stiffened me as if an electric shock was passing through. Then my thighs went weak, my knees wobbled, and my ankles shook. The jolts of those punches were telegraphed through my whole body. They sent a quick message — total destruction. I felt them down in my toes and up in my ears and in my teeth. It was as if I was standing in the middle of a terrible explosion.

I had to move. I forced myself up straight, using my open moving hands to shield off her fists. She was strong but she wasn't fast on her feet. She wasn't too smart about fighting, either. All she knew how to do was slug at her target. Pa used to say that was the dumbest kind of fighter couldn't do nothing but pound away like at an old sack of flour.

So the thing for me — the sack of flour — to do was to move.

I began to edge sideways a little, then more, to backstep and then dart a step forward when she least expected it, to dance around and even get a punch in here and there, but mostly just to stay out of the way of those fists.

I managed to yank off the yellow turban that was covering the frizzed hair — the style looked a lot better on Madonna — but before I could actually grab her hair, Lizzie punched my nose so hard, blood came gushing down. I tasted my own blood and danced away faster.

"That's for hurting my nose last time, ree-tart," Lizzie panted.

She was so big. It was like David against Goliath, only I didn't even have a slingshot or a rock. I knew I had to make a quick end to it some way or I was lost. She'd destroy me.

Suddenly, I turned my shoulder and pushed it into her with all the force I could gather, using my body to batter against her. That tipped her off balance and I pinned her in a crushing hug, and we went down together onto the pavement.

She was so much heavier, it was nothing for her to push and rock and move till she was on top, straddling my waist, knees pinning me to the sidewalk while her hands slapped away at my head and chest.

Lizzie's face was flushed and sweaty, and her eyes were dark and mean; she wouldn't stop for nothing. I understood that if I was going to save myself — maybe even from getting killed because Lizzie didn't seem to know what she was doing anymore — I would have to move very fast.

From Pa and Will Junior both, I had heard about strategy. They said it was important. That was how David beat Goliath. I could never beat Lizzie by being stronger. I wasn't stronger. I had to surprise her again in some way and get the better of her before she did me in.

My lips were dry, and the taste in my mouth was hot and salty.

I readied myself.

I lifted my legs high in the air and brought my feet in, turned so the loafers slapped like a pair of cymbals against my enemy's ears. I rocked up twice that way, fast. Wham! Wham!

Lizzie was stunned. Before she recovered, I rocked again sideways violently and pushed her over onto the sidewalk. In seconds, I was on top of her, holding one arm tight and twisting it behind her back. "Who's a retard?" I panted.

There was no answer.

I tightened the twist on the wrist. "Who's a retard?"

"No one. Leggo my arm."

"Who?"

"No one."

"Say 'I am a retard. And my mother and my father — and all my kin going way way back are like that. Even my dog — ' "

Lizzie wriggled, but I was hurting her arm too much for her to be able to do anything.

"I — am — a — retard. Leggo."

"And my mother — " I helped her.

"And my mother."

"And my fath — "

"And my father — "

"And all my kin going way back are like that."

"Andallmykingoingwaybackarelikethat — " Lizzie's words tumbled out of her mouth. "Leggo."

"Even my dog — " I gasped.

"Don't have no dog. Leggo."

"What do you have?"

Silence.

"What do you have?"

"Parakeet."

"Even my parakeet — " I insisted.

"Even my parakeet — "

"Don't call me nothing after this, or I'll get you," I told her. I kept my voice soft, FURIOUS like Ms. Walker's. "I mean it, Lizzie." I let go her wrist and climbed off. My legs were real weak and unsteady, and my fingers were bloody, but I didn't show Lizzie any sign of hurt. I stood tall as I could.

Lizzie turned herself over and she lay there on her back, rubbing her wrist and her arm. I had really twisted skin.

I watched over her. "If you ever mess with me again, I'll *kill* you," I said. "I got a knife — " I held my hands in front of me about a ruler length apart — "about yay long, and I swear the next time you bother me, I'll get you."

"I'll tell Ms. Walker," Lizzie spat out at me. "She don't tolerate no fighters in her class."

That made me boil.

"LaVerne will beat you to it. Just don't mess with me anymore, Lizzie, because I'm right handy with my knife," I lied. I really liked this picture of myself, even though I didn't even own so much as a nail file. "I got lots of cutting experience back where I come from. You just make a move against me one more time and you'll see."

I didn't wait for her to answer.

I turned my back, and — it was real hard to make every move — I managed to hurry across and away from her.

I just about made it back home before I collapsed.

EIGHT

*"Oh Lord so powerful with all Your might
Don't let LaVerne talk about the fight."*

I prayed it all the way to school. No hiding out this morning. No more 007 stuff. I walked in the open.

Trip day. I was wearing my blue-and-white-checked-blouse, all ironed nice and crisp, and a navy skirt Aunt Lottie had sewed for Sunday School. My left sock had a big hole in the heel. I had to slide it under so it wouldn't show. Now the bunched sock rubbed every step I took. These were my only matching socks and I couldn't mend them because my fingers were too sore to work a needle.

Washing the supper dishes last night had hurt worse than the fight did. I had to keep biting my lip so I wouldn't cry out from the pain, but I couldn't trouble Aunt Lottie, whose veins were so swollen she couldn't stand on her feet. She took to bed, first time since I came to live with her.

When Goldfinger wanted to find out about "Operation Grand Slam," he didn't need to stretch 007 across a table all tied up. If he made a couple of cuts in the secret agent's fingers and then dipped them in soapy dishwater, even 007 couldn't hold out. Never.

Lucky for me Aunt Lottie was lying in her bedroom, her legs raised up on a pillow. I ran cold water in the dishpan and used only my fingertips to hold things and wash them. Afterward, I had to manage to keep my hands out of sight. Aunt Lottie was too taken up with worry about her legs to notice anything much.

My fingers looked awful, as if a dog had been chewing on them. Those were the only outside marks of the fight. This morning I was wearing my old blue wool winter gloves to hide the scratches. I was going to keep my hands in my skirt pockets as much as possible. All the rest of my body was sore and tender, and my chest pained when I breathed in because Lizzie had really pounded me there as if she were trying to cave all the bones in. But the hidden injuries didn't matter. The only thing that mattered was what showed.

Did Lizzie believe me about the knife?

Did LaVerne tell Ms. Walker about the fight?

Outside the classroom, I stopped just long enough to pray my rhyme once more with all my might.

"Oh Lord so powerful with all Your might
Don't let LaVerne talk about the fight."

Then I hurried in and took my seat and looked around secretly for clues. LaVerne was right in her seat, turning pages in a picture book. Did she tell on me? She looked up and smiled. I felt hope. Maybe she didn't.

Ms. Walker and Ms. Ames, our student teacher — wearing high-heeled red boots to match her beautiful red suit — were busy checking who was there and getting ready for the outing. They both said good-morning when I came in. Ms. Ames added, "Don't you look nice in blue. Blue's your color, Ada." I would have told her green was really my color — Mr. McCoy said so — but they were really busy planning.

They didn't know! LaVerne didn't tell! Hallelujah!

"Why you wearing gloves?" Maureen asked me. Maureen was older than the rest of us, and so tall she didn't fit in her school seat comfortably, but she had trouble remembering what we learned. She got her period every month regular — she always told us about it like it was some surprise — but she couldn't even spell her own name right. I liked talking to Maureen. It was like talking to a sweet baby.

"The gloves match my skirt. Besides, my fingers are cold."

"Oh." Maureen nodded as if that made sense, even though it was so pleasant out in the early spring weather no one needed heavy clothes.

Anyone could tell Maureen anything. I could tell her I was the secret Queen of the Amazons, those fighter-women with only one breast each they told about on TV, and Maureen would believe me. There are some pretty weird things on TV.

I don't think I'd be willing to give up one breast — if I ever get any — even to be a great woman warrior. Nope. If mine grow, I'm keeping them right on me. Still, I could fight pretty well if I had to. Now Lizzie knew that. Maybe she would carry her evilness elsewhere, and leave sixth-graders alone.

The bus ride to Lincoln Park was a very long one. Ms. Walker had been drilling us on bus manners. *Let people off the bus before you get on. No yelling. No gum popping. No changing seats or needless moving around. No standing if there are any seats, except if a very old or handicapped person gets on. Then, offer the seat and stand quietly. No rude remarks. Keep your eyes on the teachers so you'll know what's happening.*

Some of the girls had been to Lincoln Park, but no one in our class had ever been on a school trip to the zoo. Today I was just like the rest of them; the first time for us all. I loved the bus. It took us through all different neighborhoods, and all kinds of different-looking people got on and off, all ages, all sizes, all shapes, with different-colored skins. Chicago was like a rainbow of the world. Some of the people looked real poor, but others had beautiful clothes on, and pearls and gold jewelry.

When we got off the bus, we lined up and walked in pairs to the zoo. There Ms. Walker said we could break the line and go about looking at the animals on our own, just like grown-ups. We had to promise to remain in that area, and we weren't to take up with any strangers. Of course, we weren't to go away with anyone. Just look and enjoy ourselves. When she blew two blasts on her whistle, we were to come right back to the starting point, near the polar-bear pool. Then we'd all move on.

The sun shone down on us. I never saw my classmates smile so much as that morning. Some kids went off in twos and threes, but I really wanted to go by myself. There was so much to see, so many different kinds of people and animals and smells (not all good) and a lovely park. It was like traveling to a new planet. In all the time I'd been in the city, this was my first real adventure!

The park was like pretend country — a little bit like home because of its greenness, except we had hills and woods, too. Pigeons swarmed over the ground as I started to walk, and once in a while I took a few running steps just to cause them to scatter. I found a straight strong branch and took it for a walking stick, the way I used to with Pa and Will Junior.

My excitement and joy in being there made me feel swollen up, ready to burst. Me — Ada Garland — I was on a school trip. I rode on a bus all the way to this great zoo. My fingers burned, but that didn't matter.

We had only a little bit of time, and there was such a lot to see. I felt I could spend a week, a month, a year in this zoo. I could live here and learn all about each animal. I could watch the gorilla and see if he really was a vegetarian, or if he sneaked meat to eat. And I could see if he was a good father the way Ms. Walker said. I could try to figure out some way to test the elephant's memory. One thing I would never do is the bull test. No, I would never wave a cloth of any color at a bull.

I tried to walk fast so I could see a lot. In the Great Ape House I came upon some of my classmates, laughing and enjoying what they saw. There were twenty-three gorillas living there.

Twenty-three! Some of the babies were real cute.

Ms. Walker had warned us against feeding or bothering the animals. "Stay back away from the ledges and the cages," she had repeated a million times. "If you go too near, you're moving into the animal's territory and he'll fight you." She told us some stories about people who got hurt, or even killed, teasing the animals. "Admire them and leave them alone. Anything else is cruel."

So, though Maureen made silly faces at the gorillas — stretching her mouth with her fingers and popping her eyes — and several others called out rude things to the Papa gorilla about his behind, and Jessica said being a vegetarian was what made him ugly, and everyone cheered when a big gorilla peed, we were all behaving pretty well as zoo visitors.

After, I moved on to watch the deer from China with backwards antlers and big feet. Then I saw the Spectacle Bear, who's got marks like eyeglasses around his eyes. Mr. McCoy would like to hear about him, I thought. And that reminded me that I'd promised to look up the hyena.

First I'd have to find him.

In the monkey house, a man in a park uniform was hosing the floor of the monkey cage. I thought I'd just go right up to the railing and ask him the way to the hyena, but the two monkeys were so funny, chattering and screeching and jumping all about way at the top, I just stood and watched till the cage was flushed out clean.

"They 'fraid of drowning?" I asked the man.

He was big and round-faced, pink-colored like a tomato not quite ripe.

"Naah," he said. "They can't drown in an inch or two of water, and they're smart enough to know it. They just don't like me to come in and clean up their cage." He smiled up at them. "If I didn't clean it regular, they'd be throwing the dirt at you and the other visitors. Monkeys don't have no manners."

"You'd think their mothers would teach them something," I said, the way I'd heard grown-ups say.

The zoo-man laughed. "The mothers are worse than their babies. One thing about monkeys: They don't learn better manners when they grow up. The older they get, the worse they get."

I decided I would put that in my composition about the zoo if I really managed to write one. Ms. Walker said I could if I made up my mind to it. Writing was getting a little easier for me, though I still had bad days when some letters came out backwards.

The zoo-man pointed out the direction of the hyena cage — down the path, then turn to the right.

I thanked him and went right off in that direction. And there it was. I walked up to the sign and squinted in the sun. H-Y-E-N-A. Some days the letters, when I was trying to read something, practically called out the word to me. That was reading! It was recognizing, and other people did it easy.

HYENA I read. Today was a good day.

Then I looked at the hyena.

It was a scruffy-looking, snubby-nosed kind of dog. I waited impatiently as the hyena paced back and forth, back and forth, sniffing as if he had a cold and looking at me as if I were in the cage and *he* was visiting. He didn't make one single sound.

You better laugh soon, I thought, so I can hear you, or I won't be able to wait. I've got to go fast.

He was not only ugly, he was contrary. I waited a while longer, then — after checking around to be sure no one else was near — I put my head forward, as close to the cage as I dared, and whispered, "Mr. McCoy sends regards to you and says for you to keep on laughing, no matter what."

At the sound of my voice, the hyena moved his head to a side as if he were measuring me, but he didn't break his pacing or make a sound.

Dumber than me when I first came to Chicago, I thought. I was disappointed, so I turned to leave. Maybe the hyena's laugh was a legend. I took two steps and then heard this weird sound — real wild laughter that made me shiver. I looked back at the hyena, but all he was doing was pacing and staring back at me.

The hyena's laugh made me nervous. It was a crazy noise, frightening in its loudness. Or maybe I was upset by the idea of a creature everyone (except Mr. McCoy) despised that kept on laughing. Mr. McCoy sure had funny taste in animals.

I was set to move out of there when two big boys came in. I lingered to see if the hyena would laugh at them.

"Laugh, stupid," one boy ordered.

They called out all kinds of mean and dirty names at the animal, who was walking back and forth and looking right at them. It didn't make a sound.

The tall, skinny boy had some pebbles in his pocket and he began to toss them at the hyena's head, aiming for the eyes. "C'mon, laugh," he called. "Laugh!" He kept pelting the animal in its face.

"You're not supposed to do that," I said.

"Who's going to stop us?"

"You're just not supposed to hurt him. It's the rules."

"What's he, a cousin of yours or something? I see the family resemblance," the fatter boy said. His head was shaved clean like an egg, and he was pretty funny-looking himself. Then he noticed my walking stick. "Lend us your stick a minute," he said.

"No," I answered.

"Lend us your stick." He moved up on me,

both his hands out. "I only want to tickle him a little. I won't hurt him."

"No," I said, backing out the doorway. I was standing in the sunlight on the stone step.

The two of them came after me together, and though I pulled them down with me I held onto my stick. They turned it back and forth, twisting it, trying to get it free, hurting my poor hands and tearing those old blue gloves so that my fingers began to bleed again.

Some kids in the class must have been walking nearby because I heard them yelling, "Fight!" Girls came flying from all over. "Here comes the teacher!" Jessica screamed, and just like that those boys were gone, running scared.

By the time both teachers were there, I was sitting up and still holding tight to my stick.

Ms. Walker just walked up close to me and bent over. "Oh!" she said. "Those poor hands." Then she asked very softly, "What happened, Ada?"

"They were bothering the hyena."

"And?"

"I told them to stop."

"Why didn't you come tell Ms. Ames or me?" I shrugged.

"Why didn't you call a zookeeper?"

I really couldn't say. When it happened, I didn't think of doing anything other than what I did.

"You must have been fighting a long time, Ada.

Your hands are badly cut. How did they ever do that through gloves?"

I shrugged. I couldn't answer that one.

LaVerne answered. "Lizzie did that to her."

"Lizzie? When?"

LaVerne was upset. She wasn't a snitcher, or she would've told before. She wanted to help me, but she didn't know how. "Lizzie ripped her hands yesterday. She was waiting on Ada after school."

Ms. Walker's voice was dangerously quiet now. "You fought Lizzie yesterday, and you didn't tell me?"

"I wanted to come to the zoo more'n anything."

"Who really started the fight yesterday?"

"Lizzie. She was waiting. And she said things — about my aunt and my mother and all my folks from the mountains."

"Who hit first?"

"She *said* things. Nasty things. Terrible things. So I had to hit her."

Ms. Walker spoke loud now, in her ANGRY voice, for the whole class to hear. "I do not take fighters on class trips. Ada will not come along next time."

She reached over to help me up, taking my two bloodied hands in her own. "Let's get you tended to," she said sadly. "Ms. Ames will supervise the others."

And once I was cleaned up and bandaged at

the medical station, she kept me glued beside her all the rest of the time till we went home.

I knew I had spoiled the trip for her, and I was so sorry. I just couldn't figure out what else I could do.

NINE

Next day I didn't *personally* conduct myself to school.

In fact, I made up my mind never to go to school again if I could help it. I stayed locked up in the apartment, watching TV programs from the minute I opened my eyes. I ate my cornflakes and drank my milk in front of the TV, and even when I washed and went to the toilet I left the door open so I could at least hear. I just wished Aunt Lottie had enough money for a set in every room. Jessica, who was always bragging, said her family did, and they kept them all turned on all day. But you could never tell when Jessica was lying. I didn't believe she had *all* big-sized color TV sets, anyway.

Today it would've been nice to have a screen and a voice talking in every room to block out bad feelings.

There was a giant sadness inside me, a lostness, same as I'd carried into this city when I first came. Grover, Bert and Ernie, and Big Bird couldn't drive it out. Their fooling around didn't even touch it. The TV shows were all stupid, and the people talked much too much. When a hamburger commercial came on, I felt dizzy and nauseous and I ran into the bathroom and threw up in the toilet. A few times during the long morning I found myself crying, even when there wasn't anything sad happening. Just a warm wetness like a drizzle kept starting up in my eyes.

A little after three o'clock, *General Hospital* came on. It was so boring — going on and on about how even though he was blind, Tony saw Charlene's shadow walking past him — I tried all the other channels, but there was nothing better so I turned it back on. During a cat food commercial with a lot of purring, there was a knock on our door.

Aunt Lottie's rule was not to open for anyone when I was in the house alone. Never. Just call out to whoever was out there to come back in the evening if he has any business with us.

The knocking kept on going, loud.

"Ada?"

I jumped up off the floor. The voice was muffled. Was it Lizzie? She didn't believe me about the knife!

In my socks I tiptoed toward the door, mindful

to go round the loose boards. I covered my mouth so no one could hear my breathing, and I waited.

"Ada Garland. I know you're in there. Please open the door, so I can speak to you properly."

I stood frozen.

Ms. Walker.

No question. Unless my ears were playing tricks, that was definitely Ms. Walker's voice. And Ms. Walker's language.

Ms. Walker standing right outside my house door. Come to track me down in my own house for playing hooky.

"Ada. Please don't keep me waiting out here in this dark hall."

In a rush now, I unchained and unlocked the door and I opened it. I peeked out and once I saw who it was, I opened it as wide as it would go. There, in her purple-and-white polka-dotted dress and purple high heels stood Ms. Walker, like a movie star come to visit.

"Ms. Walker?"

"Hello, Ada. May I come in?"

"Sure. Come on in."

The teacher walked into our living room. Two nurses were arguing with each other on *General Hospital,* and a skinny patient was reaching her hands out for someone to help her, but Ms. Walker didn't pay any mind to what was going on.

"You should have come to school today, Ada.

We missed you. Not only because the chalk-boards look terrible, and they do. Only one monitor really knows how to do a good job with them and that's you."

I kept my eyes on the TV screen but I was listening to her every word. I just didn't know what to say or do. Ms. Walker didn't sound CROSS or ANGRY or FURIOUS. She sounded normal.

"You sick?" the teacher asked.

I shook my head.

"Fingers okay?"

"They hurt, but they're healing. That's not why I'm home."

She waited.

"I was scared to come," I got out at last, "because — "

"Because you were ashamed." She finished my sentence for me, quietly. "I figured as much. Good thing I stopped by."

I didn't know where to put my eyes. I kept them on the TV.

"Look, Ada. You did some foolish things. You got into a fight, and then you deceived me. And then you got into another fight."

I nodded. It was all true.

"I can't spend my life saving Ada Garland from fights. *You've* got to do it. But that doesn't mean you're not in my class. I'm not angry with you. You're still my student, and you belong in school.

"Ada, you're just beginning to do things. You're reading. You can't stop now. You have good ideas. You can't just give up because of some foolishness."

I kept bobbing my head.

"Will you be there tomorrow? Can I count on you?"

"Yes."

"Ms. Walker."

"Yes, Ms. Walker."

She looked around our living room and her eyes took in all of Aunt Lottie's plants. "Your aunt has the most beautiful coleus I've ever seen," she said, going over to study the bright red- and violet- and green-patterned leaves.

"Aunt Lottie says the plants keep her in mind of her girlhood back in the mountains, when the world was green and blue and all bright colors."

Ms. Walker smiled. "This is a nice, homey room. Do you help to keep it so neat?"

"Yes, Ms. Walker. I do the chores. Aunt, she works."

"Well, she must be mighty proud of you. This place looks spotless."

I had to laugh. "Aunt Lottie's pretty fussy. She always finds some dust hiding somewhere."

Ms. Walker smiled, too. Then she unzipped her black leather briefcase. "Since you weren't in school for our discussion of the trip to the zoo" — she stopped talking to search among her papers — "I brought you a book of pictures of all the zoo animals and their names. There's some information about each one printed on the back of each picture. That's harder to read, so you can try it or not as you please. Keep the book here as long as you like and enjoy it."

It was a giant-sized, shiny red book with a gorgeous raised-cover picture of a tiger looking like he was about to leap out at the reader.

"Thank you, Ms. Walker." I wished she could stay. It was such fun to have company in the house in the daytime. Especially my teacher. "Isn't he a beautiful tiger?" I really loved him.

"He is an exceptional animal, beautiful and strong."

Funny how that word *exceptional* kept popping up. Before a few months ago, I'd never heard it once. Now everyone used it all the time.

"I'd like to be like him," I said, "beautiful and strong."

Ms. Walker reached out and smoothed my hair. "You can be," she said. "You're beautiful already, and you're learning how to be strong. Smartness is people's strength."

"I want to be smart more than anything."

"Well, I think you've got a good head on those shoulders, Ada. I truly do. Don't waste it. Come early tomorrow morning. Soon as you finish the boards, we've got things to do."

She stood fast for a minute. "I have homework

for you. Tonight after supper, I want you to turn off that silly tube with all those phony doctors running around like their heads ought to be operated on, and all those smiling fools trying to sell you a bunch of junk.

"You sit down and look at each picture in the book and the name that goes with it. Then you get yourself a picture in your head of each name and the way its letters fit together, along with the picture of the animal the name belongs to. See" — she flipped the book open — "SKUNK." She held her nose and she spelled out the name "S-K-U-N-K. Now sound it with me. SK-UH-NK."

I giggled, but kept my eyes on the letters. "SK-UH-NK."

"Fix the groups of letters for a few animals — not too many — in your mind. Tomorrow we'll have a little quiz. We'll go over the ones you studied to see what word pictures stayed with you. In a few weeks you might know the name of every animal in the book and be able to recognize it in print."

I couldn't think of anything to say. I already knew SKUNK. I'd never forget it.

"Shall we give it a try, Ada?"

"Yes, Ms. Walker."

"Good-bye, then."

"Bye, Ms. Walker. Thanks for coming."

"You're welcome, Ada."

I went out into the hallway to watch her go down the stairs. In the second-floor darkness, the dealer missing some teeth was hanging out, waiting for customers. When he saw her coming down, a dressy black lady with a leather briefcase, he didn't offer her stuff to buy. He didn't wait. He moved out. Too bad. She would have told him something!

She looked back up at me. "Remember to lock the door," she called and went on down and was gone.

I went right in and locked the door. The TV doctors were talking about poison. I walked up to that set and clicked it off so I could look at my book in peace.

When I finished going through it one time, I decided to take it downstairs and show it off to Mr. McCoy. I could go down there now because it was after school hours, and I wouldn't get into trouble over playing hooky. I'd tell him I hurt myself accidentally with a broken glass in the dishpan when he asked about my taped fingers. That's what I told Aunt Lottie, and she believed me.

"This is one exceptional book your teacher loaned you," Mr. McCoy agreed after we'd looked at every single picture. "I don't know when I've seen such fine animals." He folded some brown paper to make a good tight cover for the book so it would stay clean.

"Now I have to study the names of a few and fit them to the right animals in my head. Then I can recognize the names whenever I see them. Ms. Walker thinks I can do it."

"Sure can. Why not start with five animals? Five is a nice round number. Then — tell you what — I'll test you."

He sat on his broken-back chair to work at his workbench, and I settled on the hassock, concentrating so hard I began to sweat, though the basement wasn't too warm at all.

BABOON
BEAR
DEER
GIRAFFE
HYENA

First I studied each picture. Pictures never made trouble for me. They always stayed the same on the page, and I kept them in my mind. That was how I knew even before the eye test that the trouble was not in my eyes. I could have told them that. My eyes were sharp and steady as could be. It was my mind that was dim and shaky.

Ms. Walker said there were lots of people like

me, and many of them could learn except they gave up too soon. Because it's too hard.

When I knew the picture by heart, I came to the trouble part. I looked at the letters BA-BOON, and I tried to see them as a picture. BA-BOON. The two O's were like eyeglasses between the B and the N. I said it to myself, closed my eyes and tried to see it in my head, spelled it out, pointing to each letter, and then I said it again and again, my eyes first open, then shut, then open again. "BA-BOON. Eyeglasses. BA-BOON."

Slowly I did it with each of the five words, sitting there hunched up on the old hassock, working harder than I'd ever worked on school stuff before.

By the time I got to HYENA I was very tired, but I pushed on through. My head was beginning to bang like a drum. "HY," I memorized, "like when you meet someone. HY-ENA." Like I would meet a kid named ENA. HY-ENA.

"Mr. McCoy," I said, when I had all that fixed in my head, "this word HYENA reminds me that I gave the one in the zoo your regards."

"You did? What'd he say to you?"

"He just laughed a crazy laugh behind my back."

"Knew I could count on him."

"Mr. McCoy, he sure is funny-looking. And he smells. How come you want to take notice of him?"

"Can't always go by looks or smell, Ada. I think he's pretty remarkable. Nothing else like him. Let's see your book. There must be some interesting points in here about hyenas."

"Naah," I said.

He turned some pages and began to read, his finger running line by line right across the page. His lips moved a little, but he didn't make a sound.

"HYENA," he read out loud at last. "Comes from the Greek *hyaina* or she-pig, hog. Hyenas are big and powerful animals once thought to be only cowards and scavengers.

"Scavengers means they ate the flesh of already-dead animals," he explained. "Hmm. Modern scientists have discovered that hyenas are capable hunters and not cowards at all.

"They are sociable and live in packs of as many as one hundred."

He was reading to himself again. Now I wanted to hear more.

"Well, what do you know!" he exclaimed. "Live and learn. Hyenas have manners. They always greet each other by licking one another's face or by kissing one another."

"Yuk," I said.

"Heck. French people been doing the exact same thing for centuries," Mr. McCoy said. Puckering up his mouth funny, he made sounds into the air. *"Bon jour,"* he said, and made more funny sounds. "That's two French people saying hello. Ada, you ready with your five reading words?"

I nodded. I stood up. I was too excited to sit still.

"While you were studying, I printed them on cardboards. Now I'm going to shuffle the cardboards all around like a giant deck of cards, and you get to choose any one you want and read it."

I shut my eyes tight and picked a cardboard, then turned it over. A hard one. "GI-RAFFE."

He made the okay sign with his finger and thumb.

I picked another card. Eyeglasses. "BA-BOON!"

"Roger."

"DEER."

He kissed his fingers into the air with pleasure.

"BEAR."

He grinned. "Only one left now. This one's easy. My mascot."

"HYENA," I said, without hardly looking.

"Ada, you study those five before you go to bed, and again tomorrow morning when you get up, and you'll knock 'em over in school. And if you keep going, you'll be the readingest kid they ever saw in that old school. They're going to have to send that retard label right back to the manufacturer — for good!"

TEN

In the Church of the Holy Light they were always shouting about the Power of Truth, but I knew the reason Lizzie wasn't messing with me was the Power of Ms. Walker, and maybe the Power of a certain lie.

My lie — about having a knife and using it to cut people — might be what held her off. Fear. Lizzie was staying on the other side of the schoolyard because she was afraid of a cutting hillbilly.

The Power of Words was something else. Stronger than fists. Sharper than knives. I'd always loved the sounds of words, but I didn't realize their strength. I was beginning to listen all around me and I heard wonderful things from kids, from teachers, from the radio, and sometimes from the TV. Words were the music of the world.

Truth was best, I knew, but the lie was sometimes necessary, leastways in Chicago. I was sorry that I wasn't a true believer and a good Christian. I kept my thoughts to myself so as not to be a disappointment to my aunt.

Every morning I worked on my reading with Ms. Walker. We had fewer bad times with it these days. I used to look at a page and not even be able to make out the words I'd learned the day before. Now, that almost never happened. Mostly I could go smoothly for sentences and sometimes for paragraphs, surprising myself and pleasing my teacher. Each day there was a carton of milk and a straw and some cookies after I finished reading. As many cookies as I wanted! She was helping other kids other times, and they got treats, too. She said that was part of her "method."

I liked her method.

I had never felt so much hope.

Until it happened that I couldn't go to school anymore.

Aunt Lottie got sick for real.

Her legs, which had carried her for so many years, just gave out. The veins bulged as if they were about to burst, and Aunt Lottie said standing was like walking through fire. She couldn't go to work and stand all day or even sit because she said the burning didn't let up for a second.

Aunt Lottie couldn't go to work, and there wasn't money to live on if she didn't go to work.

131

The first few days we hoped it would get better. The legs had been bad before, but those times Aunt Lottie prayed and the veins healed. Jen climbed the stairs each night to leave a pot of soup for us. Not to worry, she said. Soup was a real far-spreading dish. She just added some water and a few more vegetables and there was plenty. She brought chicken soup with chicken backs in it to suck the meat off, and barley-bean, chowder, and gumbo. They were all good. Jen prided herself on her soups.

Other folks from the church came by and left cooked food, kind folks who liked and admired Aunt Lottie. They did their best, but there wasn't enough to fill me up. I was growing taller, and I felt hungry all the time. Ms. Walker had fixed me up for free lunches in school long before, but that wasn't helpful on the days when I couldn't go to school. It wasn't much fun to see TV commercials where they advertised candy bars and pizza and burgers when I was hungry.

Aunt Lottie's legs didn't get better. There was no cash coming in, no money to pay the rent at the end of the month or to pay for anything else. My aunt had spent most of her savings on the gravestone for Pa. Now she just sat all day by her plants, her swollen legs resting like watermelons on cushions on a bench. Her hands were good, so she could do her beautiful lace crochet work, and that's the way she passed the days.

She was quiet and very sad, her busy fingers working away. She didn't want the TV on, and she wouldn't allow guests to come in and visit — not even the McCoys. She was down, and said she only wanted to be let alone till she was on her feet again. The Lord was her comfort.

After two weeks of her sitting this way, the leg not improving and me missing school most of the days because Aunt Lottie woke up moaning in such pain I wouldn't leave her, Mr. McCoy climbed upstairs and wouldn't let me keep him out the door.

"I came up here to talk turkey with you, Lottie," he said severely, taking off his glasses to polish them. When Mr. McCoy polished his glasses, you knew he meant business.

"It's too early for Thanksgiving," Aunt Lottie said crossly. She was mad at him for forcing his way into her private home.

"This turkey has nothing to do with Thanksgiving and you know it."

"Send the child down to visit with Jen," she said.

"No. She belongs up here. She's getting to be a big girl, and she's a part of what we got to talk about. You can't live this way, no working, no unemployment money, and you sick. You have to get some help, Lottie."

"No Welfare — " she said, closing her lips tightly over her gums and crocheting faster.

"There's this child to think of as well as yourself. All your life you worked the best you could, and never came onto no one. Right?"

"No Aid." Aunt Lottie's needle flew in and out, pulling the ivory thread along.

"You're the most independent person I know, Lottie. If they'd a paid your Social Security and stuff all these years, you'd be cozy now and able to collect. But I know that line of work — like my own — they use us up and don't much care what happens to us. It's not your fault or mine, and it's no disgrace."

"No Welfare," she said. "I made myself a promise in church. No Welfare, never! I'd rather be a beggar on the streets. You can talk on and on till kingdom come, I won't hear you."

"You are the stubbornest woman in the world," he said in exasperation. "You going to starve?"

"The Lord will provide."

I saw she was crying.

Next morning I got up extra early, but Aunt was in pain so I made her tea and helped her with soaks for her legs instead of going to school.

About noon, I was looking in my animal book, trying to figure out the hard words on the back of LEMUR — I had worked my way through the reading and the names of all the letters up to L on the other days when I'd stayed home — when there was a sharp bunch of knocks on our door. The noise scared me because I had just read that the LEMUR was a ghostlike animal. The name LEMUR means *spirit of the restless dead.*

Aunt Lottie was startled, too. She had been dozing in her chair. "Go see, Ada," she said. "Ask who it is, but don't open the door."

The knocking grew louder.

"Ada? Ada Garland? Are you in there? Is Ms. Lottie Garland in there?"

"It's my teacher, Aunt Lottie," I said and trying to open it fast, I fumbled and took too long. At last I got it open.

"Afternoon, Ada." There she was in the sky-blue soft dress I loved.

"Ms. Walker. Come in. This is my aunt. Aunt Lottie, this is my teacher."

Ms. Walker came right over and shook Aunt Lottie's hand. "Your plants are lovely," she said. "Your room is an indoor garden."

"Thank you." Aunt Lottie looked to me. "Bring a chair, child."

Ms. Walker moved it so she was close to Aunt Lottie. "I only have a few minutes," she said. "I came over on my lunch period. I won't waste your time. Your good friend George McCoy came to see me this morning."

"Blabbermouth old man," Aunt Lottie said angrily. "Who gave him the right — "

Ms. Walker put up her hand in her cop signal. STOP! "I'm grateful to him. I knew there was some kind of trouble, of course, because Ada has

135

been absent so much, but I can't just go butting into people's affairs because I'm a teacher." She looked at Aunt Lottie, direct. "What I didn't know was that *you're* in serious trouble, and you won't take help from the people whose job it is to give help."

"No Welfare." Aunt Lottie closed her mouth tight again. She was tough.

But Ms. Walker was her match.

"You're planning to starve?" she asked. "And you're going to make this child starve right alongside you? Just to prove that you're independent? Just to prove that you're not a no-account? Who are you proving it to? Mr. McCoy knows it already. Ada knows it. I know it. The Brothers and Sisters of your church all know it. If you could work, you'd be working."

"No Wel — " Aunt Lottie started to say again, but Ms. Walker interrupted her.

" 'A man's pride shall bring him low: but honor shall uphold the humble in spirit,' " she said gently, and then waited. "Just because of your pride you are going to hurt a child who loves you and depends on you and who is really changing wonderfully."

She stopped because Aunt Lottie was crying, her body shaking with her deep sobs.

Ms. Walker dug out some tissues. "I know it's a bitter pill, but until you're well, you'll have to swallow it for your own sake and for Ada's. She's been learning and growing so fast, it's hard to recognize her. She'll be a credit to you — and to her family. She needs you to get well and be with her."

Aunt Lottie blew her nose and then blew some more, louder, but she didn't say anything back.

"The child needs a chance. The city is filled with children who need chances. Many of these children have no families to love them. Ada has you. She needs you more than anything else in life. Don't deny her her chance." Ms. Walker waited, but when she got only silence for her answer, she went on. "Do I have your permission to call Welfare and tell them there's a lady who's sick and needs some help for — for the first time in her life?"

Aunt Lottie sighed. She couldn't bring her throat to say it — I remember how that felt — so she just moved her head up and down. Then she began to cry again, bitter, bitter tears.

"Don't cry, Aunt Lottie," I begged her. Just watching made me cry, too. "Please don't cry anymore."

Aunt Lottie hauled herself straight up in her chair and blew her nose once more, real loud like a horse snorting. "No more," she said. "No more of that."

Ms. Walker got up. She noticed the crocheting

on the table and bent over to look at it. It was a tablecloth for a round table that Aunt Lottie was nearly done with.

"What beautiful work," my teacher said. "It's so delicate."

Aunt Lottie looked proud.

"Do you crochet much?"

"Whenever these hands are idle. They're idle a lot these days."

"You know, this kind of handwork sells for a lot of money," Ms. Walker said, examining the pattern of stitches front and back. "You might consider doing some of it to sell."

"I don't know a soul who'd buy it," Aunt Lottie said. "I just give it to friends or to the church, or I keep it myself."

"I know people who admire this kind of hand-work. I would buy it, for one. I love it and I can't do it myself. In fact, there are very few people who can. I think you'd be surprised at the amount a cloth like this would bring."

Aunt Lottie picked up the tablecloth and looked it over doubtfully. "You sure?"

"Tell you what. When you finish this, if you decide to sell it, send it in with Ada and I'll show it in the Teachers' Room. I bet there's a teacher with a round table who'd be just delighted to buy it and pay a good price for it, too. That is, if you aren't doing it for someone special."

"No. I was just practicing my pineapple pattern, so I wouldn't forget it. I have quite a few cloths stashed away that no one's ever used, but I can't get to them now. I just crochet for the pleasure mostly. When my eyes were better — when I was younger — I quilted."

"I sew a little," Ms. Walker said, "but only on a machine. I can't do fine work. Never could. When you have something to sell, let me know through Ada."

Aunt Lottie was thinking fast. "What kinds of things do folks like to buy — handsewn?"

"Oh, baby clothes, shawls, carriage covers, scarfs."

"Easy, quick things," Aunt Lottie said, amazed. "Bless you, Sister. You brought Hope through our door this day."

Ms. Walker took her hand. "You may not be able to manage all by yourself anymore, but if you do the best you can, then you can hold your head up high.

"Someone from Welfare will come. Don't let the questions upset you. They're nosy, but that's the way it works. You're only getting what's coming to you as a citizen."

Aunt Lottie nodded, her mind not fixed on Welfare anymore. "My friend, Jen — Mrs. McCoy — she does beautiful handwork, too, better'n mine. Do you think — ?"

"Yes," Ms. Walker said. "Of course. Gather some samples together and we'll see what's possible." She looked at her watch. "I must run. See you tomorrow morning, Ada. Early? The chalkboards are crying for you."

She was gone in a flash like a fairy godmother. Why can't a fairy godmother be black?

ELEVEN

The super end-of-the-year trip to the Hyde Park Art Fair was coming close.

Ms. Walker brought the subject up one morning during our talk before school. "Our last class trip is coming up, you know, Ada. I said you wouldn't be allowed to come because of your fighting, and I can't go back on my word. Otherwise, I won't be believed again. I just want to tell you that I know you understand how to behave now, and I trust you."

All along I had known in my heart that when the day came, this was the way it was going to be.

"You'd best stay home on trip day," Ms. Walker continued, "because if you come to school, Mrs. O'Neill will have to sit you in with a teacher who doesn't know you. There's not much point in that, so keep your aunt company at home. And please don't tell anyone I gave you this advice. I'm not supposed to recommend that you play hooky."

I was ashamed to be reminded of that zoo trip. It was hard for me to believe that I had done so many dumb things, one on top of the other: fighting Lizzie for calling me names, trying to hide my scratched hands, and finally getting into a tangle with those two big boys. Why didn't I look around for a zookeeper for some help? Why *didn't* I open up my mouth and yell? Or run for someone? Where were my brains? Not on the job, that's for sure. I was mostly living in TV-land those days.

Now I was finding I had hardly any time to watch TV afternoons. Even Mr. Rogers wasn't as interesting to me. Still nice, but a little boring. I was reading instead. Easy books. I had some hard days, but mostly I could do it, and I began to really believe that I would do more.

I wore loafers but I could tie my own shoelaces. I could even do double-knots!

I was luckier than Billy-boy. I could learn!

I joined the public library. Maybe one day I'd be able to read some of those big fat books, just read and read without one whit of trouble. Ever.

Ms. Walker gave me a present — a book of poems by white poets and black poets. First time I ever heard there *were* black poets. I could read the easy ones, and even recite a few by heart. My favorite was a very sad one, "A Brown Girl Dead," by a black poet with a funny name: Countee Cullen. I said it to myself a million times.

> "With two white roses on her breasts
>   White candles at head and feet,
> Dark Madonna of the grave she rests;
>   Lord Death has found her sweet.
>
> "Her mother pawned her wedding ring
>   To lay her out in white;
> She'd be so proud she'd dance and sing
>   To see herself tonight."

I recited it to Aunt Lottie, who leaned back and closed her eyes as she listened. "Amen," she said. "That is beautiful and religious. The Lord will love that child and take her to Him."

I recited it for Jen and Mr. McCoy and they were reminded of their poor niece, Jen's sister's girl, who died so young of drugs. "That poet could have had her in mind, it was that close to the true situation," Jen said. "Didn't matter that my niece was white. Young and dead is terrible."

The McCoys both were full of praise for all my trying to read and study. And they loved rhymes and poems almost as much as me.

"You might try writing down your own little rhymes," Ms. Walker suggested. "You might even try a poem longer than two lines. All a poem is, is a thought — or a bunch of thoughts — said in a special way. Not the ordinary way. Stronger. More beautiful. You like words so much, Ada, try a poem."

Not yet, I thought. Not while my letters sometimes switch with each other, *m* and *n* tricking me, or they jump into the wrong place so I write *becuase* instead of *because*. While that's happening I can't write poems. But if I keep practicing and doing the drills, one day maybe I will use words in my own special way and write poems. Maybe even stories. There are so many thoughts to write down, so many good-sounding words to use.

It was very hard for me to believe I was that same dummy who'd used her fists all the time to say everything. I was turning into another person, a born-again. Not in the church like Aunt Lottie wanted me to be, but a born-again person.

Night and day the trip was on my mind once Ms. Walker said I couldn't go. Till she said it out loud there was still a chance that she'd forgotten, but now that she had said it I had to accept my terrible fate because I didn't have the power to change it.

Then — on the very night before the trip — God parted the Red Sea so His child could walk across it.

Aunt Lottie said she had three fine new crocheted tablecloths — two of her own and one of Jen's — and she wanted them carried to school so Ms. Walker could see if someone would buy them.

"I'll be glad to carry them in tomorrow," I said, overjoyed. Now I had a reason to go.

It was to be a midday trip. Getting up real early, I put on my new turquoise-colored shirtwaist blouse that I'd made following a Simplicity pattern in class during sewing periods. I wore my good navy skirt and my well-shined loafers, and I made sure my navy socks were carefully mended. Even my handkerchief with its pink crocheted border of forget-me-nots was pressed.

Be brave, I told my cowardly self, and I set off for school just at the end of the lunch hour on the one day of the year I was supposed to stay home.

I didn't go right into the classroom. I stood outside the backdoor, in the hall, peeking in. The girls were all dressed up fine. Jessica, of course, was ready for a wedding in her yellow nylon puffy dress with a low-necked front and sailor collar, showing off those B cups, heeled patent shoes on her big feet that must've pinched something fierce because they were so pointy.

Everyone's hair was combed real pretty, and everyone's shoes were shined. Mine was really a good-looking class!

"Seats, girls," Ms. Walker called, taking Yolanda by the elbow and starting her in motion toward her chair.

"Ms. Walker," I called softly because she was heading toward the back near where I stood.

She heard, but she was too mixed up in what was going on to pay real attention. She looked around, bewildered, trying to track my voice.

"It's Hot Ada," Jessica announced. "She's always so hot to fight, she's staying behind today."

"Jessica" — Ms. Walker stared her right down into her seat — "so will *you* be staying here if I hear you again." She looked toward the back door. "I'll be with you in a minute, Ada. Please wait there."

On the chalkboard she wrote:

TRIP WORD LIST
    trip
    artist
    painting
    sculpture
    statue

She pronounced each word and got the class to say it after her. She told what each word meant. "Write the words in your spelling lists," she said. "Be careful about letter size. Notice there are no capital letters in this list at all. That's because we don't have any proper nouns. We don't have any *specific* names of persons, places, or things."

She stood there waiting while they took their lists out and began to work. "Get it done quickly," she said. "We want to go."

The teacher then came to the backdoor and right on out into the hall. I stood there waiting, anxious, holding the long flat white box in my hands.

Ms. Walker looked me over. She recognized my fresh new turquoise shirt. She had helped me finish it off on the sewing machine. She could see my shining loafers and my carefully combed and pinned hair.

"Afternoon, Ada."

"Aunt Lottie sent three tablecloths, two of hers and one of Jen's. They're hoping you can find customers for them."

Taking the box from me, Ms. Walker lifted the lid off and examined the stitching in the lovely ivory-colored cloths. "They're magnificent," she said. "Tell your aunt I'm positive someone will buy them."

"She'll be mighty happy."

"You know, Ada, your aunt and Jen are artists every bit as much as the people showing their stuff down in Hyde Park. Theirs is home art: learned at home and done at home. They didn't have outside chances to learn, and that used to be true for most women.

"But, now! You keep up with your schoolwork

147

and you are going to have other chances. One day, perhaps, you'll write fine poems. I really believe that."

"Thank you," I said. "I'm trying." Then I just stood there looking at her. Waiting.

"Ada?"

"Can I come, Ms. Walker?"

"I explained — "

"I won't do anything bad."

"I know you won't, Ada. But I told the class you were not going on this trip as a punishment for fighting."

"You could change your mind, Ms. Walker. A teacher can do anything."

She smiled, but her eyes were sad. "What would my word be worth around here?"

I really had no answer to that.

"Who will believe me next time?"

I cast about in my mind, desperate for something to say. I cast about for anything, *anything*! "You remember when you told Aunt Lottie, 'Just because of pride you're going to hurt a child who depends on you'? And Aunt Lottie, even if she is a sick old lady, she knew she was wrongheaded, and she changed. She let the Aid people come. She's taking Welfare money for my . . ."

My voice was disappearing on me. I could hardly make the words sound out loud. "Ms. Walker," I whispered, "Lizzie started that fight. I couldn't help it. I didn't know how to help it. She hid, waiting for me — without her shiny white jacket — because — she was expecting blood. Ask LaVerne. She — saw it starting."

I was shaking, terrified that I was becoming a dummy again. The pain in my throat and in my chest was tearing and sharp, as if my voice were being ripped out of me.

"I believe you," Ms. Walker murmured. She could feel my trouble. "I hear you." She turned and pushed open the backdoor to the classroom. "Take your place in the class."

"I won't make you sorry," I whispered gratefully. "I swear I won't."

Anyway, Maureen was glad to see me. She smiled at me and moved her long legs over so I could get by. The others were all busy writing except for Yolanda, who was busy spying. Once she saw me coming in, she pushed Jessica's arm.

Jessica looked up, and Yolanda pointed to me. Then Jessica's hand was up, waving wildly before Ms. Walker even made it back to her desk from the closet where she was locking up Aunt Lottie's box.

"Yes, Jessica?"

"You said Ada couldn't come on this trip. Why's she here?"

"I changed my mind."

"She fought them boys in the zoo. And Lizzie."

"Lizzie started that," LaVerne interrupted. "Lizzie is a addic'."

"Ada did fight," Ms. Walker said, "but since then she's worked very hard and behaved well. She's learned a lot. So I decided to give her another chance."

"That ain't fair," Yolanda grumbled.

"She's coming along. If anyone prefers not to make this trip today, I can arrange for her to stay back. Now's the time to say."

There was an uneasy quiet in the room, which was broken by Ms. Ames, our student teacher, who walked in, looking just lovely in a tan clingy dress, her blonde hair loose and wavy to her shoulders. Everyone thought she looked just like Melanie Griffith.

"Let's get the attendance," Ms. Walker said, moving fast. She crisscrossed her roll book quickly, then took out the blue one hundred percent attendance banner from her desk drawer and gave it to Ms. Ames to tack on the door. That banner only came out on trip days. Regular school days, kids cut.

We began to review the rules one last time, fast. During this trip we would have to do a lot of walking, as well as take buses. We had all been told to wear comfortable shoes and, except for Jessica, we'd obeyed. We went over sticking together, trying to walk in line if possible, not answering back if someone yelled something stupid or rude at us. On the bus, if we got seats we'd stay in them — except to give them to old folks or blind people or cripples — and we wouldn't pop our gum or carry on.

LaVerne knew all the rules. She could answer any question about trips. She looked like a kewpie doll, round cheeks and pretty lips, a babyish loose starched lavender dress with mother-of-pearl buttons down the front, and matching hair ribbons in her braids. LaVerne was really lucky: Her mother only worked part-time, and she had a live-in father and he had a job.

Ms. Ames asked, "Has anyone ever seen an art exhibit before?"

Old Jessica's hand had to fly up first. "I seen one. I seen this one already. My daddy rode us right past it in his new car."

"Well, la-de-da — " Maureen said. "That ain't seeing it. That's just passing it."

I was proud of Maureen for talking up. She didn't, usually. But she was tired of Jessica bragging all the time about *her* father and *her* car and *her* everything.

Ms. Ames put her finger over her lips, and Maureen shut up.

"I think we should get started," Ms. Walker said. "I want you all to have a very good time today. Remember to mind your manners and make Ms. Ames and me proud to walk alongside you."

Maureen, pretty in her denim skirt with patch pockets and matching jacket, was my partner.

Through the halls and down the steps we went, out into the schoolyard. Then the line halted while Ms. Walker went to the office to sign us out. Otherwise, Mrs. O'Neill might think we were kidnapped, she said. We stood, watching an eighth-grade gym class playing softball.

Lizzie came up to bat. I'm not sure it was her turn, but she made it her turn.

The pitch was way outside, but she took a wild swipe at the ball, anyway, and missed by a mile.

I was so excited and happy about going on the trip, I didn't even wish Lizzie anything bad at that moment.

Two more bad pitches. Two more wild swings, and Lizzie was out. She threw the bat aside. She was blazing mad.

"That pitcher can't throw for nothing," I said to Maureen. I was thinking that Lizzie shouldn't have swung for any of those throws. I wouldn't have swung.

"Who you talking about, Dummy?" Lizzie snarled at me.

"Dummies can't talk," I said.

"I'll see you later, Talking Dummy." Her eyes glittered with hate.

As our double line began to move slowly, Lizzie purposely stood in the way, breaking it into two files.

"Move, Lizzie," Ms. Ames said. "You're breaking our line. Girls, stay with your partners."

Lizzie didn't budge. "You're not a teacher," she said.

Ms. Walker came right up to her and stood face-to-face so close that Lizzie was forced to back off out of the way. "She's a teacher when she's working with me. You'd better respect her." She moved on with the line.

Lizzie stood very close on the side, watching us go. "I'll see you and your tight-ass teacher later," she muttered at Maureen and me. "Just you watch. I can break that uppity black teacher's li-ine if I want to. Oh, yes!"

I shrugged and walked on. Lizzie was crazy — or high — or both — to be starting up with Ms. Walker. 'Cause in her right mind, she'd know better. That's how come I'd been safe all these weeks. Maybe she was a little scared of me and my made-up knife, but she was more scared of my teacher who was my protector.

Now I wanted to put Lizzie out of my mind, for we had a whole wonderful free afternoon in front of us. What an exceptional idea an art fair was!

I felt like skipping and jumping, but that wasn't allowed. I just walked along at peace, holding tight to Maureen's hand.

TWELVE

Where was that bus? We stood and waited and leaned over on tiptoe on the curb, wishing it to come, thinking that maybe something had happened to all the buses in the city, despairing, and then it came. Inside the bus, I was surprised how many words I could make out on the advertisements. Of course, the pictures helped. All those beautiful people smoking were selling cigarettes. Made me remember my pa hunched over, coughing and spitting. Those signs lied. Smoking had nothing to do with being beautiful.

My classmates were orderly. We sat up in our seats in our best clothes, looking good, talking and giggling. I tried to be the perfect bus passenger, shoulders back, my hands clasped in my lap, holding my pretty handkerchief so the pink crocheting showed.

A tall boy carrying a basketball got on, a handsome brown-haired boy with a dimple in his chin. There was some quick seat-changing up front, first moving away from him, then nearer to him. Mostly we behaved.

When we got off the bus, Ms. Walker said we'd been terrific so far, both walking and riding, and now we had more walking to do through unfamiliar streets so we should stay close together. We had to pass through some pretty poor streets, poorer even than where we came from, projects with mostly black people living there far as I could tell. Then we got to the schoolyard and the fair.

It was like entering a shining sunlit other world, the way Dorothy must have felt in Oz. There were strange and marvelous paintings hanging all around the place, and there was jewelry, and clay pottery, and statues, and even beautiful cloth of many kinds. We were early and that was lucky because the fair wasn't crowded yet.

The artists were very friendly. There was one old man who wore a monocle. Ms. Ames said that was what you called it. It was one eyeglass over one eye. It just sat there in his cheek like a little round window. He painted autumn scenes in bright yellows and flaming reds and oranges. Some of his forest pictures reminded me of the woods back home in Indian summer just before the leaves fall, when it seemed as if nature was about to explode with its own fireworks.

Mr. Monocle went to a lot of trouble to explain to us that his paintings were reduced in price from two-hundred-fifty dollars (TWO-HUNDRED-FIFTY DOLLARS!) to twenty-five dollars. He gave little printed cards to our teachers, clicking his heels and bending over from the waist each time, like he was tipping forward. I noticed that his monocle stayed right in place when he tipped. How did he ever manage that?

"Come to my studio and watch me paint," he invited the teachers. "You make me sorry I do landscapes. I should do teacherscapes." And he winked the eye without the glass. The teachers and he laughed.

A little ways along we met a velvet artist. She was a lady with a million freckles, wearing tight red slacks that Aunt Lottie would die if she saw — Aunt Lottie didn't approve of pants on women — and she explained that painting on black velvet was a very great art, extremely hard to do because velvet is so delicate and the nap bruises easily. She didn't do landscapes. She did tiny pictures. Min-ia-tures she called them. (That means small.) They were bouquets and dolls and tiny clown faces that were kind of scary in their harsh bright masks. Her colors hurt my eyes.

We wandered past many statues and paintings, then we stopped for drinks at a water fountain. I was so thirsty, I drank and drank till Yolanda yelled I was drinking it all up, so I stopped.

The water tasted good out there in the sunshine with all the art around us. It was different from the usual water; everything was different and much better on this trip day.

A funny-looking skinny lady in a loose-hanging long white embroidered dress, which looked like her nightgown, came along looking at the pictures and walking a skunk on a leash right near us. A lot of the girls shrieked "Stink!" and ran, trying to get away from the skunk.

"He's de-scented," she said, very annoyed with us. She picked up her pet and held him in her arms like a baby and walked away from us fast, scowling.

"Never mind her. She shouldn't walk a skunk if she doesn't want to be noticed," Ms. Ames said. "She's just asking for attention."

The best part of the exhibit, for me, was the table displaying miniature clay heads. The sculptor, a pretty black woman, older than Ms. Walker, with real bushy gray hair, wearing jeans and a T-shirt, welcomed us. "You look like young ladies from the middle-school grades," she said. "My youngest daughter is just your age."

"How do you make the heads?" I asked. They were so delicate and beautiful.

"Sit down," the sculptor said, "and I'll show you."

I sat on her brown canvas folding chair, and she began rolling a tiny ball of clay in her hand.

I was nervous. I didn't know what I would do to pay because I didn't have any money, but she figured out what I was thinking and said right off, "This is a free sample for you. A present."

I was so *glad.* Some jealous talking began behind me, but I didn't pay it any mind.

"Why does *she* get it?" Yolanda asked pretty loud. "*She* wasn't supposed to even come along."

No one answered her, so she shut up.

First, she used an orange stick, which traced marks on the clay, then a toothpick, which dug grooves in it. A skinny, flat tool the sculptor called an emery board was used to smooth the surfaces, and she dug its edge into some of the features to make them deeper. The artist used her fingers to pinch the clay and shape it. At last she held it up.

It was me, a tiny clay me. A pretty miniature me. My face, my nose, my eyes, my mouth, even my hair pinned down. Me!

The kids all admired it. "Ada. It's Ada," they said.

Smiling, the sculptor gathered up a bunch of orange sticks and emery boards from her workbox, and then she broke off a big hunk of clay from the block in her bucket. "I'm going to give you some starting materials so you can all try making clay miniatures," she said. She took all this stuff, along with the clay head of me packed in a tiny box, and put it in a big plastic sack that said MARSHALL FIELD, then she handed it to me. "You carry it for your class."

"Thanks," I told her. "Thanks a lot for everything." I wished I could have hugged her, but I was too shy.

"Thank you for being so generous with my girls," Ms. Walker said.

"They could all be my daughters." The sculptor smiled.

Next stop was the ice-cream store. Ms. Walker and Ms. Ames treated us all to double-scoop cones! I chose chocolate chip. Maureen tried rum-raisin and said the rum part was making her drunk, and giggled something fierce.

We walked along in the warm golden light of late afternoon, licking our cones and staring at everything around us. I knew I would remember even the smallest details as long as I lived, and I would tell it whenever I could. It was the best day in my entire life. The zoo trip, up until the bad part — the fight — had been pretty good, but this one beat it by miles.

We made it over to the bus stop okay, and the bus came fast but it was very crowded. Ms. Walker let it go by, and then the next one, too, but the crowds were getting heavier. She realized we wouldn't all be able to get on the same bus, so she told Ms. Ames to take the first group on the next bus, and she would follow with the remaining girls. We would all wait for one another at the stop nearest the school, and then we'd link up again and walk back together.

"I want to go on the first bus," Maureen said, pulling me forward. "I'm tired, and my feet hurt."

I wanted to wait and ride with Ms. Walker, but I couldn't leave my partner. And when Maureen got tired-whiny that way, she wouldn't change her mind.

"Ada," Ms. Walker said, "you and Maureen go on the first bus with Ms. Ames and help her. Maureen, you stay right close to Ada and listen to her."

We got on the bus, but it was very crowded and hot and not clean like the one we came on. There was trash on the floor, a Sprite soda can rolled around under our feet, and there were crushed newspapers and pizza crusts. The other passengers weren't smiling and friendly to us now. They looked beat.

Four high-school boys got on and began fooling around, pushing each other sometimes into the girls from my class. Jessica took out a glossy purple lipstick and put it on heavy, without even a mirror to look into. It was too bright. She looked weird, like one of those miniature clown faces. We were all sweaty and tired and cranky, looking to get off at our stop and go home.

When we finally did get to our stop, the girls up front and Ms. Ames began to squeeze toward the exit to get off. I had to call to the driver to wait till Maureen got her foot back in her shoe, so we were the last ones off the bus. As soon as we stepped down, we walked into trouble. It was there, standing and waiting for us, all set up.

A few feet up ahead of us stood Ms. Ames, trying her best to get the kids' attention. But they were staring off to one side up ahead, way over to the right. And some of them were already on their way over there where they shouldn't have been.

What was going on?

Lizzie.

There she was near a big dead tree, hanging out with two other eighth-graders, the three of them in their shiny white jackets. I thought to myself, they don't want blood. They're just making mischief. Or else they would have left the jackets home. They were motioning with their hands for us all to come over.

"Come on, she's only a student teacher," they yelled. "We got something good for you here. Come see. Come on. You don't have to listen to her. She can't do nothing to you."

They were holding up filled plastic sacks and jiggling them.

It was too much for my classmates. They had to go see. I held on to Maureen's hand, and I wouldn't let go. "Don't go, Maur," I said. "Stay with me."

"Girls" — Ms. Ames called — "come back."

161

She was uncertain about what to do, and you could tell it by her voice. No one was listening to her. So she walked after the others.

Lizzie's voice was real loud and frantic now, Lizzie going wild. "Okayokayokayokay. Walker's little ree-tarts. We got candy for you. You like Clark bars? Nestlé bars? You want some sweets? We just liberated some from the A&P. All you got to do is jump for them. Nothing to it. Just let go your stupid partner's hand and jump. Okayokayokay."

And she leapt up on the bench and ripped open her plastic sack with her teeth, then lifted it as high in the air as she could get it and swung it around, shaking out candy bars and showering them all over the place. Her buddies tore their bags open the same way and began to scatter Milky Way bars and Mr. Goodbars.

"Okay" — Lizzie clapped her hands once, loud — "go for it, ree-tarts."

A cluster of hands went up, reaching eagerly. Then the girls bent down and went to the dirty pavement and began to scramble for the candy bars.

Lizzie and her two friends stood there, enjoying themselves. Lizzie was laughing, snapping her fingers, and rocking her body with pleasure as she watched my classmates crawling around.

"I want candy!" Maureen pulled at me, but I held on like we were handcuffed.

Then things happened fast. Ms. Ames, furious, confronted Lizzie. "Why did you do that? Why?"

Lizzie jumped down off the bench. "None of your business. You ain't nothing but a student teacher. You've got no right to yell at me." Lizzie gave her a hard shove in her shoulder, pushing her backward, and then moved toward her again.

I let go of Maureen's hand and dug in the MAR-SHALL FIELD sack till my fingers found one of those emery boards. Moving up close behind Lizzie, I pressed it right in her back. "This is my knife, Lizzie," I crooned, nice and sweet. "Remember I told you about it? My hillbilly knife?"

Lizzie stopped moving. I shoved the emery board harder into her back. Just the way she'd once dug me with her elbow.

On the corner the next bus screeched to a halt. The doors opened. Passengers began to stream off, and then kids. We could hear their voices. Ms. Walker would be last off the bus. Would she come in time? Lizzie's friends would attack in a second.

One of them signaled. "The bus! Here comes the rest of them."

Lizzie turned her head, then ducked real low to the side and bolted, the other troublemakers right behind her.

Ms. Ames was okay, her hair wild and her face red and angry, but she was okay. She tried her best to stop the scramble on the sidewalk. "Girls,

girls, stand up." They were just creeping around, picking up candy or trying to grab from one another.

"I got eleven." Jessica was happy, sitting on the pavement, her lap filled with candy bars, and her arms covering them to protect them from grabbers. She moved to cover up her bare thighs with her skirt. "Eleven! The most, I bet."

"Lucky you," Yolanda said. "I only got four. You going to share?"

"With who? You crazy?"

At last. Ms. Walker. At last.

"Girls — stand up immediately." She gave them a minute to dust themselves off. Then her eyes studied us all over. Her face had a closed look to it. No one could tell for sure what she was thinking.

"If you live close to here, you may go straight home," she said. "You need not come back to school. But I want your promise you'll go directly home."

That got her a few tired cheers.

A whole bunch of them went off, hanging close to Jessica like she was flypaper. Just because she grabbed so good. If they thought she was going to share with them, they were crazy. Maureen went along with them. She was mad that I'd kept her from going after the candy till it was too late. But she'd forget about it soon, I knew. Maureen was sweet-natured.

"Sorry," Ms. Ames said. "I'm so sorry."

"What happened?"

"Lizzie and her friends were waiting for us."

"It wasn't your fault," Ms. Walker said. She patted the student teacher's arm. "I should have seen it coming. Lizzie will have to be dealt with." Ms. Ames was about to say more, but Ms. Walker raised her hand to a full STOP sign. "Tomorrow," she said wearily. "We'll take care of it all tomorrow."

"I'm walking back to my car," Ms. Ames said out loud. "It's parked just outside the school, so the rest of you going back that way can come along with me."

Everyone else went, but I didn't want to. I wanted to stay with my teacher. I hid behind the tree.

Ms. Walker slowly, very slowly, walked over to the bench and sat down. Putting her arm along the backrest, she turned and rested her head on it, eyes turned into her arm.

"Ms. Walker," I whispered, when I felt brave enough.

She turned her head up, still resting on her arm. "Ada? You still here?"

"That Lizzie is crazy, Ms. Walker. Something's wrong with her. When she laughs, she sounds just like a hyena."

Ms. Walker just shook her head and looked sad.

"They all did just what she wanted them to," I said. "Just exactly what she wanted them to. But I didn't. I jammed this emery board hard against her back when she pushed Ms. Ames. I fooled her. I pretended it was my hillbilly knife."

Ms. Walker sat up and listened.

"I love chocolate most of any food," I said slowly, "but I didn't jump. I remembered you said to make you proud to walk alongside me. I never jumped once."

"Ada" — Ms. Walker smiled in her tiredness — "pretending that way was brave and brilliant!"

At that word *brilliant,* a warm breeze brushed my face, touched my cheeks light as a feather, and I took it as a sign. The folks in the Church of the Heavenly Light were always seeing signs of God's grace, but this was my first time. I would tell Aunt Lottie so she could rejoice.

The sign said to me: *The cold wind is gone for now, Ada. You are safe. The big hole punched in the world when Will Junior died is mostly shrunk up.*

I trembled all over with happiness, even though I knew trouble was bound to come again. Mr. McCoy says trouble is the winter season of life, and you just have to make it through the best you can in order to enjoy the beautiful spring and summer and fall. "There's much more good weather in life, Ada," he likes to remind me. "You just got to manage till the thaw."

166

Ms. Walker went on talking. "Girl, you're going to be all right. You're going to do just fine. I know it. Do you know *how* I know it?"

I shook my head.

"Because a lot of your trouble came from not thinking, from being too quick, too ready to fight. From being Hot Ada." Ms. Walker got up off the bench. "But a girl who finds her way out of trouble by pretending is something else. She's using her mind!"

I grinned at that compliment.

She brushed her fingers along the scars on my cheek that Lizzie had made when we fought. "Now, and for the rest of my life — and you must always remember I said this — whenever I think of you, in my mind you will always be Kool Ada."

And we laughed out loud together, my teacher and me.